THE
SHIMMERING

D1527662

CHRIS DOOHAN

PAGE PUBLISHING
Conneaut Lake, PA

First originally published by Page Publishing 2022

ISBN 978-1-6624-8379-0 (pbk)
ISBN 978-1-6624-8380-6 (digital)

Printed in the United States of America

Hadley Barrett went to college at the California Institute of Technology and holds two master's degrees. One in astrophysics, and the other in cosmology. He also holds bachelor's degrees in applied physics and mathematics. He's a confirmed geek and is quite proud of that distinction. Having had a fascination with space, he always knew as a child that he would follow his passion into adulthood.

We find the now forty-year-old Barrett sleeping. The bedroom in his home is exceptionally dark, with only a soft glow coming from the moonlight through his slightly open window. The alarm clock on his side table reads 2:33. A noise is heard, awakening Barrett. The noise stops abruptly, and the room is once again silent. Barrett looks at his clock. "2:30 in the morning...damn."

Barrett rises out of bed to investigate the noise. He leaves the bedroom and walks down the hallway, looking in every room while trying to remain silent so he can hear the noise again. Unable to find the source, he walks back to the bedroom and quietly shuts the door behind him. Barrett has always been a light sleeper, and once awakened, he has a hard time falling asleep again. He decides to go out to the porch to enjoy the beautiful night sky. He mutters out a few words, "My God, what a beautiful night." He can't remember seeing such a clear, star-filled night like this. It is like a blanket of stars are laid out just for him. Still looking at the stars, he ponders how he got there...thinking about his childhood.

CHAPTER 1

It was June 24: just two days after Barrett's twelfth birthday, and the last day of school before the beginning of summer vacation. It started out like any other day. He woke up, got dressed, and helped himself to the usual bowl of sugar frosted flakes. His diet consisted of two primary food groups…cereal and peanut butter sandwiches. Barrett's mom would make a lunch bag everyday with what she called the "healthy food," that would make him "grow up big and strong." Most of the time, Barrett would throw the "healthy" things into the neighbors' bushes while he was walking to school. He didn't come from a wealthy family—as a matter of fact, they were quite poor. He was an only child being raised by a single mom. She did a great job of raising him, and he never actually realized that they were poor.

Barrett was ready for his last day at school. He picked up the lunch bag from the kitchen table, kissed his mom goodbye, and walked out the door to go to school. Halfway to school, there was an empty lot that he and his friends called the "big field." Barrett would meet his friends there every day before school, then would walk to school together. The lot was so big, that it took almost fifteen minutes to walk from one end to the other, then another ten minutes of walking through a housing tract just to get to school.

Barrett had two great friends. His best friend was Fred, but everyone called him "Ladd." His other friend was John…just plain John. When they weren't at school, they would go to the big field to work on building their fort. The "cave," as they called it, was fantastic, and was completely underground. They started by digging a large hole in the ground, then covered it with plywood from Ladd's old tree house and the wood that they would find in trash cans around the neighborhood. Once they had the roof in place, they covered it with plastic tarps, and finally, the dirt that they had temporarily discarded behind a bush so no one would see it. All three of them had been working on it for months, but it was still a work in progress. This was by far the best fort that they ever had, and keeping it a secret was a full-time job.

The entrance was covered with a 4 x 4 piece of plywood that was covered with glued-on dirt and stapled-on leaves to camouflage it. Once you entered the cave, you would sort of fall into the first area, but that's where the fun began! There were three tunnels, the longest being about twelve feet. Each tunnel led to large underground rooms that they meticulously dug out. They were planning on making several more rooms if they had the time. Each boy had their own room, and each room had its own name.

Barrett's room was called "the lab" and was by far the best room in the underground fort. In that room, it was Barrett's job to conduct experiments with his chemistry set. Barrett came up with many new inventions that he knew would save the world from mass destruction.

Ladd's room was the "boardroom," where they spent most of their time. The boardroom had a small table, three chairs, star charts, posters, sci-fi toys and a huge stack of playboy books that they stole from John's dad.

John's room was known as the "observation deck." This room was essential for the fort's survival and to keep a look out for the "teenagers from hell." This band of fourteen-year-old hell-raisers would constantly pick on all three of them and would surely destroy their fort if they knew about it. The observation deck had a wide PVC plumbing tube that started out as an air vent, but Ladd added a few angled mirrors and turned it into a periscope that protruded through the ground to spy on their enemies and potential girlfriends. The big field provided the quickest way to get to school and was used by at least ten percent of the school kids, so keeping an eye out for danger was a constant job…and a tough one.

John would always ask if he could switch rooms, but Ladd and Barrett insisted that he was the best man for the job.

CHAPTER 2

On the way to the cave, Barrett met up with Ladd and John.

"Hey…we better check the cave," Barrett said.

"Yeah, those A-holes better not have touched it," said Ladd.

"Oh yeah, like you could do something about it," John said.

Both Ladd and Barrett replied simultaneously, "Shut up, stupid."

They got to the entrance of the cave and looked in all directions to make sure no one was around. It appeared that the coast was clear, so Barrett slid the opening to the side and looked inside to see if everything is okay. Meanwhile, John and Ladd were checking the camouflaged periscope hidden next to a bush. Everything looked okay, so Barrett slid the door back in place and kicked some dirt on top to hide the edges.

He turned to the guys. "It looks okay, guys! It doesn't look like anyone has touched it," he said.

John replied, "The periscope is down...looks good too."

Ladd gave the thumbs up. "Cool, let's go. We'll meet here after school...well, that's if Barrett doesn't have a date with his girlfriend."

Barrett shook his head and rolled his eyes.

"Oh, Kimmie, wherefore art thou, Kimmie," John said with a chuckle.

"She's not my girlfriend, dirt-wads," said Barrett.

The boys left the cave and headed through the field on their way to school.

All three boys entered their first period science class and sat next to each other. Both John and Ladd were fooling around, but Barrett was focused on the blond-haired, blue-eyed Kimmie who sat in front of him. The teacher began talking about Einstein's theory of relativity.

"Einstein's theory of relativity shows how matter…" She stopped talking abruptly because she noticed Ladd talking. "Fredrick…is there something you want to share with the class?"

"Yes, Mrs. A," said Ladd. "Barrett was just telling me that he and Kimmie would like to be transferred to the sex education class."

The whole class started laughing, and even Mrs. Arlington cracked a smile. Barrett and Kimmie were mortified and embarrassed.

Mrs. A raised her voice. "One more outbreak like that, and you'll be spending the rest of this class in detention," she said.

"Yes, Mrs. A… I'm sorry," Ladd replied.

The rest of the school day went pretty much as planned, but all three boys were excited about summer vacation. The bell rang, and school was finally out. The boys jumped out of their seats and ran out of class so fast, that you would think they were being chased by a swarm of bees. They slowed down once they reached the parking lot and started walking home.

"Dude, sorry about that sex education thing," Ladd said, slightly out of breath. "But you've got to admit, it was pretty funny."

"Yeah, at my expense…real funny! You only wish she liked you," Barrett said in exasperation.

Ladd was about to say something witty when he noticed the teenagers from hell sitting near the cave.

"Oh crap!" he said.

"What," said John and Barrett simultaneously.

Ladd pointed to them while moving behind a tree for cover. Both John and Barrett saw what Ladd was pointing at.

"Crap is right…do you think they've seen it?" said Barrett, as he and John moved behind the tree with Ladd.

"No, they would have destroyed it by now," said Ladd. Barrett agreed.

"We need to distract them to get them away from the cave before they see it," Barrett said, followed by a momentary pause. "I got it! John, you need to walk ahead of us and let them see you! Once they do, start running towards your house. I know they'll chase you."

John was not really embracing the whole idea of being a decoy. "Oh, that's a good plan," he said sarcastically. "No friggin' way, dude!"

"What makes you think they'll chase him?" said Ladd.

"Are you serious? They hate John," said Barrett.

Ladd agreed. "Yeah, you're right…okay, John, get going."

"Come on guys, they'll kill me!" John said, while thinking that his friends were throwing him under the bus.

Barrett tried to quell his fears. "They'll never catch you, and you could outrun anyone of those guys. Plus, you'll have a head start," he said.

"Yeah, once you're near your house," said Ladd, "They'll stop and probably go to their own hangout."

"Alright, you guys, I'll do it, but if they catch me, you'd better come help me!" He agreed to reluctantly.

Both Barrett and Ladd replied together. "Done!" they said.

"Awesome…we'll stay behind this tree and meet you at the cave in thirty minutes. If you're not back in a half hour, we'll start digging a nice spot for your body…okay, go!" said Barrett.

John started walking down the path, pretending not to see the teenagers from hell. Buck, the biggest of the teenagers, saw John.

"Dudes…check it out! What are the chances of this…? Our little friend is walking all alone, without his annoying buddies!"

The other teenager from hell, Kevin, said, "Let's get him!"

The teenagers started running towards John. In the corner of his eye, John saw them and starts running as if his life depended on it. He started pan- icking, but then realized that he did have a substantial lead and the chances of them even getting close were unlikely. With the teenagers clearly out of sight, Barrett and Ladd followed close behind to make sure John was alright. John appeared to be out of harm's way, as they can see the teenagers from hell walking the other way. Barrett, with an I-told-you-so look, said, "I was right…as always. Let's go to the cave."

"I'll race you," said Ladd.

Ladd and Barrett were running full steam and made it back to the cave in less than a minute. "I won!" says Ladd, panting like he ran a marathon.

"Well, at least you're good at something," Barrett said, laughing while trying to catch his own breath.

Barrett reached down to pull off the 4 x 4 piece of plywood on the cave entrance. Both boys jumped inside.

Barrett reached up to slide the door panel shut and turned to Ladd. "Geez, why is it's so warm in here."

"Got me," said Ladd. "Maybe we hit a vein of magma and didn't know it?"

Barrett, laughing, said, "I think we would know it, dork-weed. Come on, let's start digging the tunnel in our new room."

Barrett and Ladd grabbed their small shovels and a few buckets to hold the dirt, then proceeded to crawl through the tunnel to get to the lab area. "Dude, it's never been this hot in here…go over to the observation deck and open the vents," said Barrett.

"Make sure the coast is clear… I'll start digging." Ladd agreed.

"Alright, I'll get more batteries for the flashlights too." Ladd started crawling away toward the observation deck while Barrett started to dig. Ladd entered the observation deck and pushed up the periscope. He looked in and turned around, making a complete 360-degree turn. He knew he needed to do this in order to see the entire field. "The coast is clear!" he yelled to Barrett. Ladd carefully opened the vents, then starts looking for batteries.

The place was a mess, and he was having a hard time finding them. Plus, it was not his room, so he was not that familiar with it. He also found himself distracted by all the Playboy centerfolds on the cave wall. Suddenly, he heard Barrett yelling at the top of his lungs…like he struck gold.

"Ladd… Ladd! Get in here…hurry!" Ladd rushed out of the observation deck, tripping and bumping his head along the way.

"I'm coming!" he said. Ladd entered the lab, stood up, and saw what Barrett was looking at. His mouth and eyes were wide open.

"What the heck is that?" he said. The object was metallic and slightly curved or convex.

"Dude, I think we found buried treasure," Barrett exclaimed. Ladd was not that optimistic.

"Maybe it's a car or a dishwasher that was buried here a long time ago…touch it!"

Barrett was a little weary about touching it, but said, "Okay." He slowly reached out his hand to touch it and got about one inch from it when John entered the room.

"Hey, what are you doing?" he said. Both Ladd and Barrett were startled. They jumped up and screamed.

"Oh my God…don't you ever knock? You scared the crap out of us!" said Barrett.

"Oh yeah, what the hell am I going to knock on…dirt?" John was looking at the object on the wall of the cave. "What the hell is that?" he said.

"I think it's a dishwasher or something," said Ladd. Barrett, with a look of total disbelief, said, "It's no friggin' dishwasher, Ladd." Barrett again reached out to touch it. "It's warm," he said.

Ladd, now with a confused look on his face, "How the hell could it be warm?" he said. "It's been buried underground in cold dirt."

"Let me touch it!" says John. He reached around Barrett and touched it in the exact place where Barrett touched it. "That's no flipping dishwasher!" he said.

"Brilliant deduction, Spock," Barrett said. "We need to dig around it and pull whatever it is out."

The boys started digging around the object as fast as they could when Barrett heard a noise. Whispering, he said to the guys, "I hear someone outside. Be quiet... I'm going to go take a look." The boys kept digging as Barrett entered the tunnel. He got to the observation deck and slowly raised the periscope, putting his face in so he could see. He turned it and saw the top of someone's lower back, so he carefully and quietly raised it a bit more.

It was Kimmie with her best friend, Brittany. They were standing only five feet away from the periscope directly on top of the cave. Barrett was thinking to himself, *Man…she is so beautiful.* The two girls were talking as Barrett listened in mid conversation.

"Yeah, I know. Buck is a jerk…but what do you think about my neighbor, Barrett?" Kimmie asked.

"He's cute, but why does everyone call him Barrett? Is that his last name?" she asked.

"Yeah, I think so," said Kimmie. "I don't even know if he has a first name. The teachers call him Barrett too!"

"That's weird," said Brittany. "It's probably something stupid like Dracula or Poindexter."

"He's no Poindexter," said Kimmie with a smile on her face. Brittany looked at Kimmie, just realizing that she may have a crush on him.

"Ew…a bit defensive, aren't we? Hey, I heard about the 'sex education' thing in Mrs. A's class today. That must have been pretty embarrassing?" said Brittany.

"Yeah, it was…do you think he likes me?" said Kimmie.

"Dah! Only the whole school knows that!"

"Cool," Kimmie replied. "We'd better get home before it gets too late."

The girls got up and walked away. Barrett watched until they were completely out of sight, then pulled the periscope down and sat there, contemplating what he just heard. "I can't believe she likes me," he whispered to himself. Barrett had a smile a mile wide on his face as he crawled back to the lab. He entered the room, and John spoke out, "Who was it?"

"No one," Barrett said while looking at the object.

"Wow, what the hell is that thing?" he said.

Ladd replied, "We've decided that it's a spaceship that crashed landed here one thousand years ago, and that Scotty is still inside trying to get the dilithium crystals to power up."

"Very funny, ha…ha. Anyway, it's getting late. I didn't tell my mom that we were hanging out, so I better get home," said Barrett.

Ladd agreed, "Yeah, I better go home too… but first, we've got to make a pact not to tell anyone about this, at least until we know what it is." They all agreed and shake hands.

"Let's all meet back at my house tomorrow morning at nine o'clock, then we'll come back to the cave and start digging around this thing," said Barrett. They all agreed and crawled out of the cave. Barrett put the door back and threw some leaves and dirt on top, then they all headed for their homes.

CHAPTER 3

It was 12:45 a.m. and Barrett was in his bed, staring at the ceiling. He couldn't seem to think about anything, other than what he saw in the cave…and maybe a little about Kimmie. He sat up from his bed. "I'm going," he muttered to himself. He got out of bed and put on the same clothes he wore that day. He didn't seem to care that his jeans were still dirty from working on the cave earlier. Dressed, he walked over to his closet and pulled out a jacket and flashlight. He opened the door and slowly walked out. The floor was creaking, so he decided to go back into his room. The last thing he wanted was for his mom to wake up and catch him, so he carefully opened his window and crawled out. His room was on the second floor, but luckily, the sturdy wooden trellis worked well as a ladder…as he knew from sneaking out in the past.

Barrett was a little afraid of the dark, but he felt compelled to get back to the cave, so he ran as fast as he could to get to the field. Once there, he shone the flashlight at the cave entrance, slid it to the side, and got in. "Geez, it's still hot in here," he mumbled. Barrett removed his jacket and headed down the tunnel toward the lab. Halfway through the tunnel, his flashlight started flickering off and on, then went completely off. Expecting it to be dark, he was surprised to see that he could see almost everything. He looked in the direction of the lab and noticed a glow. "Oh crap, we must have left a candle lit." He proceeded to the lab, looked in, and was surprised to see that the object was glowing. His first response was that of fear, but it quickly turned to astonishment. Now on his knees, he slowly shuffled over to the object. As he did, the object started to vibrate, releasing dirt from all sides.

"This is definitely not a dishwasher," he said. As quickly as the vibrations started, it stopped. Barrett sat there stunned and amazed, and for whatever reason, he was not afraid…and he was conscious of that.

He sat there for a moment, then slowly reached out and placed his index finger on it. "Nothing," he muttered. Still glowing, he reached out again, but this time placed his whole palm on the object. Again, nothing happened. His mind was a flutter about what this thing could be. Suddenly, the object started vibrating again, but this time much more vigorously. Barrett took his hand off and backed up, putting his hands on the ground behind him. "This can't be good," he said. The object shook even more violently, bringing dirt down everywhere around him and knocking down his chemistry set.

"Oh crap, I'm out of here," he said with a louder voice. Barrett was worried, and for good reason. The whole cave may collapse on top of him at any time, so he raced to get out. Halfway through the tunnel, he noticed that the vibrations stopped. He looked back and saw that the object was still glowing. Still, he felt like he had to get out. Just as he turned to leave again, he heard a voice… "Stay."

"What? …did you say something?" Barrett replied. Barrett went back into the room and sat again in front of the still glowing object.

"Hello, is there anybody home?" He heard nothing at first, then a loud voice startled him. "Need help!" The object glowed brighter as it speaks.

"There's no way that this is actually happening…you need help? What are you? Who are you? …

how do I help?" Barrett replied. He sat there for what seemed like forever, but got no response to his question. Not knowing what exactly to do, he decided to start removing dirt from around the object. After about ten minutes, he saw what looked like a door of some type. "My God, Ladd was right, this is a spaceship!"

Barrett was extremely excited, and still, surprisingly, not afraid. "Can you hear me...do you still need help?"

The ship spoke again, "Stay." Barrett couldn't help but smile. *Am I actually speaking to an alien?* he thought to himself. "I'm here... I'm not going anywhere. What do you want me to do?" he said.

Again, the ship said, "Stay."

Barrett replied, "Crap, this is getting old. Can you say anything else?" A few minutes passed without the ship saying anything. "If you don't say something, I'm leaving." He waited another minute for the ship to say something, but still no reply.

Impatient, Barrett got up and said, "Alright, I'm leaving!" He turned around like he was going to leave when the ship spoke again… "Touch." Barrett was thrilled and thought to himself how clever he thought he was. *Yes, Mom's child psychology books really paid off.* Barrett reached out to touch the ship on what appeared to be the door; again, with his whole palm stretched out.

The ship began to shake again, but not as violently as before. He kept his hand on the ship as the door began to slowly open. Nervously, he blurted out the words, "Oh shit!"

Not a second later, the ship said, "Shit." This put Barrett at ease and made him laugh a little. With the door only partially opened, he took his hand off the ship. As he did, the door stopped opening. He placed his hand back on the ship, and the door slowly started opening again. Barrett realized that it didn't appear that the door would open without his touch. "Come on, baby…open up!" he said, keeping his hand on it.

After a few minutes, the door was fully opened. Barrett peered inside, but it was too dark to see anything. He picked up a small dirt-clod and threw it in. The dirt-clod came right back at him and hit him in the head. "Hey, that hurt," he said to the ship.

The ship repeated, "Stay."

"Oh no, we're back to this again…you really need to work on your vocabulary. I hope you don't think I'm going in there?" said Barrett.

The ship again replied with "Stay."

"You want me to go in there, don't you? Listen, you seem like a nice spaceship and everything, but there's no way I'm going in there alone." Barrett had a thought. "Hey…my friends are meeting me here at nine o'clock in the morning. They can go in there with me!"

Almost being interrupted, the ship loudly said, "FRIENDS, NO!"

Barrett replied, "Friends, no? …friends, yes! How do I know you won't eat me the second I walk in there? Hey, listen, I've got to go home. My mom will kill me if I'm not in my bedroom in the morning, but I promise I'll be back later…okay?"

Again, Barrett heard nothing. He left without any comment or resistance from the ship.

CHAPTER 4

It was early morning, the first day of summer break. Barrett was in his bed when he was awakened by both Ladd and John, yelling in the front yard outside Barrett's window. "Dude, wake up! It's the first day of summer vacation," Ladd said.

John spoke in a high girl's voice, "Barrett! It's me, Kimmie. Can you come out and play?"

Barrett opened his window and looked out. He was clearly excited to see them and couldn't wait to share with them what he experienced in the cave. "Guys, I'll be right down. Have I got something to show you!" Barrett ran down the stairs and straight out the door. Unfortunately, in his excitement, he forgot to put clothes on and was wearing only his underwear briefs. Both of the boys were laughing and pointing at him.

"Yeah, you've got something to show us, alright!" said Ladd.

John, still in his girl voice said, "Oh, Barrett, we haven't even had our first date."

Barrett looked down and was clearly embarrassed. He turned around and ran back inside. He got dressed, but this time with clean clothes.

Barrett ran back to his friends, and all three of them started walking to the field. Barrett was dominating the conversation. "Guys, I swear. I was at the cave last night, and the thing started glowing and shaking…the dirt was falling all over me! Then… I swear, there was a door that just appeared. The door opened, but it was really dark inside, so I threw a dirt-clod inside. Then something inside threw it back at me! It totally wanted me to stay, but I needed to go…"

Ladd interrupted, "Wait, now it talks? Hey, John, the refrigerator talks!"

"I think Barrett has finally fallen off the deep end," said John.

Barrett, knowing it sounded crazy, said, "Okay…just wait until you see it…you'll eat your words."

The boys got to the field and looked around for the teenagers from hell. The coast was clear, so they entered the cave. Barrett led the way. "Follow me," he said with excitement. Ladd and John were still laughing as they crawled through the tunnel. John and now Ladd were talking in a high-pitched voice. "Barrett, will you hold my hand? I'm scared."

"Oh, me too," said John, "I don't know when I've been more frightened."

Barrett shrugged them off. "Keep laughing, shitheads," he said.

The boys entered the lab and could see that more of the object was uncovered. John saw that it had a roundish shape, but couldn't see any door or glowing. "It's a friggin' sewer pipe," John said.

"Well, that explains why it's warm. So, where's the door and the voice?" said Ladd.

Barrett looked and felt very confused. It looked nothing like it did last night. John spoke out, "Quiet... I hear something!" The boys were silent, trying to hear what John heard. John tried to speak in his best alien voice. "Take me to your leader."

They all thought it was funny...well, except for Barrett. "I swear, guys, this thing was glowing and talking, and there was a friggin' door right here!" He pointed to the side of the object. "All I did was touch it and it opened."

"Then touch it again," said Ladd.

"No, let me do it," said John. John reached out and put his hand on the "sewer pipe."

"I don't feel anything....wait! I feel a vibration!" Both Ladd and Barrett's eyes widen. "Oh my God!" said John.

"What...what?" said Ladd. John kept his hand on the object for a few more seconds, then yelled, "IT'S GOT ME... HELP! HELP!" Both Barrett and Ladd screamed in reaction. John turned his head toward them with a smile on his face.

Barrett, realizing it was a joke, said, "You A-hole."

"I knew he was going to do that," said Ladd.

"Oh yeah, right! Your face turned as white as my butt," said John. Ladd turned to Barrett and put his hand on his shoulder.

"Buddy, I don't know what you think you saw last night, but this is a sewer pipe." In order to save face, Barrett decided to tell the guys that he was just kidding about the whole thing.

It was now obvious that whoever or whatever was in this ship did not want anyone else to know. "I know," he said, laughing. "I was just messing with you guys... Got ya!"

"I knew you were kidding all along," said Ladd.

"Well, we obviously can't dig a new tunnel in this room. I guess we'd better do it in your room, Ladd," said Barrett.

The boys spent most of the morning digging their new tunnel in the boardroom. Barrett looked in occasionally at the object, but nothing happened.

Done for the day, they completed their exit checklist by making sure all candles were out and the flashlights were off, then at the last minute, checked the perimeter using their periscope. Before leaving, all three boys grabbed a bucket full of dirt, took it outside, and dumped it behind the bushes. This was something they've done hundreds of times, and it was the one time that they were the most vulnerable to detection.

CHAPTER 5

Barrett walked up the stairs to the porch and opened his front door. "Hey Mom, you home?" He got no answer. Barrett's mom worked as a bank teller full-time and sold real estate when she had free time... which was rare. She inherited the house, but still needed to work two jobs in order to pay the bills, so she was almost never home during the day. Barrett had been a latchkey kid for many years, so he was quite comfortable being home alone.

He entered the kitchen, grabbed some crackers, and fed his pet parrot named Terd. A friend of Barrett's owned the bird, but gave it to him when he had to move across country. He renamed it Terd after the first time he had to clean his cage. After taking care of Terd, he turned on the radio and opened the refrigerator. The song "I Feel Good" by James Brown was playing. Barrett picked up a spoon and pretended it's a microphone. "I feel good. Da, da da da da da da…like I knew that I would now da da da da da da da!" Still singing, he grabbed the jar of peanut butter off the shelf and helped himself to a big spoonful. "Like sugar and spice….so good, so good…"

Kimmie was walking up the path toward Barrett's house, carrying an empty cup. She stepped onto the porch and heard him singing. Looking through the window, she saw Barrett singing and dancing around the kitchen. She was smiling and thinking about how much she liked him, but knew how embarrassed he would be if he knew she was watching. She kept watching for a few more seconds, then knocked on the door. Barrett turned his head and saw Kimmie at the door. "Oh my God, it's Kimmie!" he said under his breath.

"I'll be right there," he said. He put down his spoon, but didn't realize that he had a small amount of peanut butter on his lower lip. He walked up to the screen door.

"Hi, Kimmie!"

Kimmie pretended that she didn't see him singing and tried to ignore the peanut butter on his lip. "Hi, Barrett. My mom wants to know if we can borrow a cup of sugar?"

"Um…a…sh—sure," Barrett stuttered. He opened the screen door and reached his hand out for the cup. "Just give me a second," he said as he was walking back toward the kitchen. He got the sugar and returned.

"Thanks!" she said.

"Not a problem," said Barrett.

"Hey, Barrett!" she said coyly, "Me and a couple of friends are going to 31 Flavors tomorrow…do you wanna go?"

"Sure," he said with delight.

"Great, I'll see you there around 3:30?" she said.

"Okay, see you then…that should be fun," he replied.

Kimmie waved goodbye and walked down the path. She was almost home when she dumped the cup of sugar on the ground, clearly using it as an excuse to ask him out. Barrett was back in the kitchen with a smile as big as the Cheshire Cat as he packed some food to take to the cave. He was talking to his parrot, Terd. "Terd, this is an awesome, stupendous day! I've not only been asked out by the prettiest girl in school, but I found a spaceship in the big field!"

Terd looked back at him with an incredulous eye.

"Oh, you think I'm nuts too…you're just a stupid bird."

CHAPTER 6

Barrett's mom was pulling into the driveway. Barrett saw her and quickly hid his bag of food that he was preparing to take to the cave, then ran out to help her with the groceries. "Hi, Mom! Can I spend the night at Ladd's house tonight?"

His mom looked at him with one eyebrow up. "Hi… I missed you too. Didn't you spend the night at Ladd's house last Friday?" she said.

Barrett replied, "That was three weeks ago, Mom!"

"Alright," said his mom, "but you need to clean your room first."

Barrett hugged her, grabbed a bag of groceries, and took it to the kitchen. He helped his mom put away the groceries, then grabbed his hidden food bag and went back to his room. He started cleaning his room while at the same time packing his sleeping bag, food and jacket into his backpack. He didn't usually pack a sleeping bag when staying at a friend's house, so he opened his window and dropped his backpack into the bushes, so his mom wouldn't question him.

Barrett had no plans to actually spend the night at Ladd's house. The sun was almost over the horizon, so Barrett said bye to his mom, headed out to pick up his backpack, and started his walk to the cave. He entered the field, and again, looked in every direction to see that no one saw him. He slid the cave door open, got in, and took out his flashlight before making his way to the lab.

The room was warm and glowing again as he spoke to the ship. "Why didn't you glow like this when we were here earlier?"

"Friends no!" the ship replied.

Although Barrett was a little worried that he may have to do this alone, he was happy to hear the voice again. At this point, he had no idea if this voice was an actual alien, the ship, or a robot inside the ship. Barrett took off his jacket, as there was no need for it in the warm cave. "Okay…do you want me to come inside?"

The ship replied, "Touch." Barrett reached out to touch the ship close to where the door appeared earlier. With his hand on the ship, the door suddenly appeared next to it. It began to open.

"Here we go!" he said. The door was now completely open. Barrett removed his hand and just sat there in front of the door, thinking that something may come out, but it didn't. The inside of the ship was dark.

"I can't see anything. Can you turn a light on?" he suggested. He was just about to point his flashlight inside, when the inside of the ship began to glow off and on, but not as bright as it was on the outside. "That's better. Not perfect, but better," Barrett said as he peeked his head into the craft. "Oh my God, what happened to your ship, and what in the hell is that smell?"

Barrett couldn't see much, but enough to see that the ship was cluttered with all kinds of stuff. He tried to turn on his flashlight, but it didn't work. Then, seemingly coming from the middle of the ship, he heard, "Stay please."

"Where are you?" said Barrett. He decided to take a leap of faith and entered the craft…slowly. He put one leg in, then the other, thinking for a moment that something may grab him and pull him in, or eat his feet as an appetizer. He grabbed the inner part of the door with his hands and cautiously pulled himself inside. He looked around the ship and was amazed by the technology he saw, but also slightly disgusted by the mess.

The craft was beautiful to Barrett, regardless of the mess. Smooth round metallic surfaces of many colors, with lights and panels that revealed strange but beautiful designs. He stumbled over to a panel that looked like it has alien writing on it. "What does this all mean? Are you here?" He heard nothing. He turned his head to look at the other side of the ship and saw what looks like a dirty glass window. He went over to it and used his hand to wipe off the dirt. At first, he saw nothing, but then looked up and spotted something, but couldn't quite make it out.

He cleared more dirt off the glass and looked in again. Startled, he screams at what he sees. "*AAHH!*... is that a skeleton? Is that one of you guys?"

"No, Barrett," said the ship.

"You know my name?" Barrett said.

The ship replied with a "yes."

Barrett still wanted an answer to his question. "Whose skeleton is that?"

He got no response. He decided to investigate the glass again, then realized that there were several glass enclosures throughout the ship. He rubbed the dirt off another glass enclosure and saw a smaller skeleton resting on the bottom.

Bewildered, he said, "Why are these skeletons everywhere...and where are you?"

Then, from the center of the ship, he heard, "Barrett friend."

"Yes, friends, but a friend would answer my questions though," he said with frustration in his voice.

"Here," the ship said.

"Here where?"

The ship repeated, "HERE!" with a little frustration in its voice.

Barrett, not knowing where "here" was, began moving towards where he believed the voice was coming from. At the center of the ship he found a coffin-like glass tube lying horizontally on the floor, partially sunken within the floor. The glass was foggy, but he did see a strange vague figure inside. "Is this you?" he said.

"Yes."

Barrett was happy that he found him, or it, but wasn't sure what he could do to help. "Earlier you asked me for help…what can I do?"

"Touch." It said.

Barrett touched the tube, just as he did when he was outside the ship. It started to glow and shake. Barrett could see that it was moving slightly and noticed that it appeared like it may be breathing. Barrett spat on his sleeve and started wiping the glass. He again looked inside to get a better look. "Hey, you're kind of creepy-looking."

"Stay…touch." Barrett stayed and kept touching the glass. There was more movement inside, so he tried to clean the glass a bit more so he could see the whole alien.

He glanced again and saw that the alien has a large thick tail, small arms and hands, and eyes that came off its body that resembled a hammerhead shark. The alien inside began to speak, but it now seemed to have a stronger, more confident voice. "Thank you, Barrett."

"Are you okay?" said Barrett.

"Now better. More energy," it said.

"I have so many questions to ask you…did you crash here? How long ago?"

"Time is irrelevant."

"By the look of this place, I'll bet it's been twenty or thirty years!" said Barrett.

"One hundred and two earth cycles," said the alien.

"One hundred and two years! Man, are you old!"

"Age irrelevant," said the alien.

Barrett really wanted to help him, but felt helpless to do so. "Can I help you get out of this thing?" he said.

"I must stay here for now. Need more energy."

"How do you get more energy?" Barrett asked.

"You," he said.

Barrett shook his head in disbelief. "I was afraid you'd say that," he replied.

"My name is Fobo, from planet far away. Our species learned long ago that certain beings through-out the universe are gifted with a life-giving energy. You are one such being, Barrett. We also learned how to harness this energy to run our cities, homes, and even our spaceships."

"Me! …are you sure? I don't feel very powerful," he said, perplexed.

"I'm sure, Barrett," said Fobo.

Barrett's mind was blown and couldn't really grasp the reality of what Fobo just said. "Why are you here?" he asked.

"My purpose was to bring these special life-forms, we call Fayrons, from other worlds to be placed on our home planet. These creatures were to bring the life energy back to our dying planet. My mission was almost complete, but when travelling close to your planet earth, my ship was struck by an asteroid…that collision killed or seriously injured most of the Fayrons on this ship. The crash on earth left me as the only survivor. It was the Fayrons that gave this ship its life. I have been unable to depart due to lack of that energy. If it had not been for you, Barrett, I may have never completely awakened."

"You've been asleep for 102 years?" Barrett said.

"My body…yes," said Fobo.

"So, you are kind of like Noah with his ark?" Barrett asked.

"Our purposes are not dissimilar, Barrett." Fobo paused for a moment. "Your friends are approaching."

CHAPTER 7

Both Ladd and John were walking and talking in the field on their way to the cave to look for Barrett. "Barrett told his mom that he was staying at my house tonight," said Ladd.

John giggled. "Maybe he's in the cave with Kimmie."

"No way," said Ladd, "Barrett would never tell anyone about the cave...not even Kimmie."

The boys got to the cave with flashlights in hand as Ladd slid the door open. John looked inside. "I don't think he's in here...it's pretty dark," muttered John.

"He's probably hiding, getting ready to scare the crap out of us," said Ladd.

"Barrett! Are you in there?" John yelled. The boys dropped themselves into the cave and went through the tunnel to enter the lab. They looked around and saw that everything was pretty much how they left it. The spaceship still looked like a sewer pipe, just as before, but Barrett was nowhere to be found.

Barrett, inside the ship, saw his friends through the hull of the ship as if it was completely transparent. He could see and hear everything they were saying, almost as if he was directly in front of them. Barrett moved closer to the boys and yelled, "Guys, I'm right here!... Guys!" He turned to Fobo and asked him, "Why can't they hear me?"

"They must not know, Barrett," he insisted.

Barrett was clearly frustrated and couldn't understand why Fobo was keeping him from his friends.

He turned back to the boys and started pounding on the side of the ship where the boys were. "Come on guys, I'm right here!" He got no reaction from his friends, but regardless, kept pounding on the ship wall. Realizing that Barrett wasn't in the cave, both Ladd and John started to leave.

"They're leaving, Fobo. Please let them stay!" he pleaded.

"I'm sorry, Barrett," he said without emotion. Barrett sat down on the ground, exasperated and feeling defeated.

"You're not going to let me out of here, are you?" he asked.

"Barrett, you are the only chance for my survival. I need your energy to escape your world, and to save mine."

"Can't you find someone else?" asked Barrett.

"There are only twenty-eight Fayrons on your planet, and only three of them are human. You are one of only two Fayrons in what you call the United States. Before I crashed, my sensors picked up a Fayron directly below the ship. I used almost all the energy the ship had to crash near that Fayron. That Fayron was your great-grandmother. The gift was inherited by her firstborn...your grandfather. Your father was a Fayron."

"Did my dad know he was a Fayron?" he asked.

"No... Most Fayrons do not know. He passed it on to you when he died, as you will do upon your death." At this point, Barrett's mind was in meltdown overload, but he seemed to find the courage to continue.

"How do you know so much about my family?" he asked.

"I have been with your family for 102 years. It was essential for my survival. Their thoughts and your thoughts, have become my thoughts…and my thoughts have become yours. Both your fascination with astronomy and even building this cave were mental transfers from me to you. I learned your language from your ancestors."

"Mental transfers… You mean telepathy? …this is too weird!"

"Barrett, I will need your help to get home. I cannot force you, or hold you against your will, but if you do not stay, I will certainly die."

Barrett paused for a few seconds to think. "Well, since you put it that way, I guess I don't have much of a choice. What about my mom and Kimmie? Oh no! … I have a date with Kimmie tomorrow!" he said with exasperation.

"You will return before your mother ever knows that you are gone…and I would never let you miss your date with Kimmie."

Confused, Barrett asked, "How is that possible?"

"I will explain at another time, Barrett. We have much work to do. I will need your assistance to make repairs."

"Repairs!" he said roguishly. "What you need is a maid."

CHAPTER 8

Barrett helped clean up and make some repairs to the ship under Fobo's guidance. Fobo wasn't able to help with much of the physical work, but did assist Barrett and told him how to fix things. Barrett left the ship for a short time to get a bucket to put the bones in. While he was putting them in the bucket, he thought about how cool it would be to bring these to school for show-and-tell, but knew he could never do that. He took the bucket and dumped the bones in a hole inside the lab, then covered it up.

It was now 6:22 a.m. and the major repairs were complete. Barrett felt pretty good and proud about what he had accomplished. "Not bad for a twelve-year-old…huh, Fobo?" he said.

"Not bad, Barrett. We must leave soon. The power needed for graviton to graviton lift will leave us visible until we leave Earth's atmosphere."

"This ship can become invisible?" says Barrett.

"With adequate energy, I can alter perception, making the ship look like a flock of birds, or almost anything else. This is how your friends believed my ship was a sewer pipe. I was able to store just enough energy when you were close to the ship…thank you."

"Cool! Do you need me to sit somewhere for takeoff…like an energy sucking chair or something?"

"It is not necessary, Barrett. Sit anywhere… We will leave in three minutes."

Barrett looked around, but saw no chairs, so he sat on the floor. The inside of the ship started lighting up. There were beeps, whistles, and a deep thunderous humming coming from beneath his feet. He was too excited to be scared at this point. All he could think about was space travel and how he never thought he would ever be in space. Just as he was beginning to get comfortable, Fobo spoke, "Your friends are approaching."

"Should we wait to take off?" Barrett replied.

"We cannot."

"I can't believe I'm going into space. This is a dream come true."

"I know, Barrett," said Fobo.

"Of course, you do," said Barrett.

The ground around the ship started to shake as the ship slowly rose. John and Ladd were almost at the cave when they felt the ground shaking. "What the heck is that…an earthquake?" said John.

Ladd looked ahead toward the cave as the ground started to swell. "Look at the cave!" he said.

Inside the ship, Barrett talked to Fobo. "This is the coolest thing ever! Is there a window?" Fobo put his finger—one of only three—on a small button. The window appeared. "Whoa, there's John and Ladd!"

The ship rose out of the ground as dirt, plastic tarps, and plywood were falling off the top. The spacecraft was oblong and oval-shaped with nothing attached. It, too, was metallic looking, with a beautiful opal-looking hull. The boys stood there frozen, with their mouths and eyes wide open. The ship hovered for a moment, then jet out to space at an incredible rate of speed. "This is unbelievable, Fobo," Barrett said. He looked out the window, which was now much larger. He saw the earth below him and was silenced by its beauty.

"We must prepare for transfer."

"Transfer…what the heck is that?" said Barrett.

"We must travel to a world that is over one hundred light-years from earth. This can only be accomplished through inter-dimensional transfer. We must collapse and bend space-time to shorten the distance."

"Cool! We learned a lot about space and physics in Mrs. A's class."

"I know. You should hold on to something." Fobo completed the countdown. "Three...two... one!"

The ship increased speed as Barrett held on with both hands. The ship traveled through a tube-like cloud with every color in the rainbow. Barrett saw several other galaxies, planets, and solar systems passing by, almost as if you were watching a movie in fast motion. Then the ship came to a complete stop. Barrett was stunned by what he was witnessing.

There was a star, an orange dwarf, and several planets in view all around him. Barrett turned to Fobo. "Gnarly! Which planet is yours?" he said.

Fobo replied, "None of these are Ramar. My planet was even more beautiful than these…and it will be again."

"I thought we were going to your planet?" said Barrett.

"We will…in time. I must do my best to complete my mission first, Barrett. It is very important."

"You mean we need to go alien hunting first?"

"We never hunt…we ask or suggest that they join us."

"I know, Fobo, I was just messing with you…so which planet are we going to go to?"

"The second planet from its star…this is the first planet that is in the habitable zone."

"What is the habitable zone?" questioned Barrett. "The habitable zone is an area that is not too close, and not too far away from its star. A planet must be in that zone where it is warm enough to have liquid water, which is needed to support life on its surface. There is life on many other planets that are not in this zone, but life there only exists in subterraneous caverns."

"That makes sense... I guess," said Barrett.

The ship traveled past two planets and an asteroid belt. Fobo kept the ship at a comfortable distance from it, for obvious reasons. The ship stops approximately two hundred miles above the planet, "Tayth." The planet was similar to Earth, but with much smaller oceans.

"This looks like a pretty planet," said Barrett.

"Tayth is pretty, but primitive and dangerous. Many of the creatures there are large and carnivorous. We must locate a Fayron that is neither."

"How do we do that?" questioned Barrett. Silently, Fobo waved his hand over the control panel next to his cryogenic tube. A holographic-like image of the planet appeared in the middle of the room next to Fobo. Red dots were seen sporadically around the planet.

"Are those dots where the Fayrons are?"

"You learn fast, Barrett. We must choose one of these. This planet has thirty-eight Fayrons. We may take only two. It is important to leave a large, healthy population of Fayrons. They are needed for its survival…you may choose, Barrett."

Barrett looked at the image and could not decide. After a few moments, he pointed to one near the planet's equator. "Done! …you may want to sit down, Barrett."

CHAPTER 9

The ship began to enter the planet's atmosphere. Barrett watched through the window as the ship traveled through the dense cloud cover. They started to slow down and found themselves just above a thick jungle canopy. "The Fayron should be directly below us," said Fobo. The ship lowered itself through the jungle canopy and landed near the edge of a cliff with waterfalls and lush vegetation.

"This place is great! Is the Fayron out there somewhere?" Fobo began waving his hand again over the control panel.

"Yes, it should be very close. We will send out a probe to take a closer look."

"A probe!" Barrett said. "let me go out there instead?... I can find it."

"You may be able to find it, Barrett, but I'm worried that it may find you first. I am picking up patterns that concern me."

"What do you mean...it may be aggressive?" he said.

"Yes. We must let the probe do its job first," said Fobo.

"Like I said," said Barrett, "Let's send the probe out there first."

Suddenly, there was a noise coming from the back of the ship. Out came a mini version of the ship, but with arms and an area that looked like an eye at the top. It measured about eighteen inches in diameter. "Wow, you're full of surprises, Fobo. This is totally cool. What's its name?"

Fobo turned to Barrett. "His name is Terd," he said.

Barrett started laughing. "Ha ha, no way... that's the name of my parrot!"

Fobo cracked a smile. "I know... I liked that name," he said.

Fobo spoke to Terd. "TERD! FREMAK TARAS BEBARO TAMATRI SIMYEK."

On command, Terd flew through the hull of the ship, as if there was no hull there at all. Barrett looked on in awe of the alien technology.

"That's a nice trick," he said to Fobo.

"We will see what Terd sees...look over here." The wall next to Fobo turned into a live image of what Terd sees.

"Terd vision...very cool, Fobo," Barrett said with amazement in his eyes. Terd continued to travel independently and autonomously through the jungle canopy on his search for the Fayron. He came across a small creature in the trees and moved in closer to examine it. The creature had a frog-like face and was hanging upside down on a branch by its three prehensile legs. It had two long arms which looked way too long for his body, and it appeared to be reaching out to Terd. Terd reached his arm out to touch the creature's hand.

"Hey, is that the Fayron... How do we get it?"

"I'm afraid that's not a Fayron, Barrett. Terd's sensors are picking up no traces of Fayron energy in the creature, but I do sense that it is close."

Fobo gave Terd another command. "TERD... FREMAK TARAS BERIBI," he ordered. Just as Terd received his new orders, the frog-like creature was swept away by something very big, hitting Terd at the same time. Terd was knocked down to the planet's wet surface by this large creature.

"Oh my gosh, what happened...is he in the water?" questioned Barrett. Terd, seemingly okay, turned his vision up into the tree.

"The small creature has been eaten," said Fobo.

"By what?" said Barrett.

Terd's vision focused on the large creature, clinging to a branch high up in the tree. It had almost completely eaten the frog-like creature, and all that could be seen out of his mouth was the arm that was tenderly reaching out to Terd. Barrett was a little grossed out by what he was witnessing. "Oh man... look at that thing! That has got to be the ugliest lizard I've ever seen!" The lizard-like creature was huge and appeared to be at least twelve feet long and at least two feet wide, with several mouths and arms. It didn't appear to have eyes of any kind.

Fobo reacted. "Unfortunately, I believe that is our Fayron. Terd's sensors were very active when he was hit."

Joking, Barrett said, "Hey, I'm not related to that thing…am I?" Fobo apparently didn't think that remark warranted a reply, so he remained silent. With Terd vision still on, they noticed that the creature was making its way down the tree towards Terd.

"Fobo, it's going after Terd!" Barrett exclaimed.

Fobo sent emergency orders to Terd. "TERD. REEFLAKI… REEFLAKI!" The orders didn't get to Terd in time as the large creature jumped on top of Terd, swallowing him whole.

"Oh no…he ate him," said Barrett, "What are we going to do?"

Fobo didn't seem worried, as he kept his eye on the screen. They both looked at Terd vision and saw what's inside the creature's stomach…including the not yet digested remains of the small frog-like crea-ture. Barrett opened his mouth and stuck his tongue out, pretending to throw up. "This is totally gross!" he said.

"Don't worry, Barrett…this is a Fayron being. Terd is clever and is using this opportunity to take an advantage. He is storing much needed energy."

"Great, but how the heck is he going to get out of there? …and if he does, I'm not cleaning him!"

Fobo turned to Barrett. "Terd has a few good tricks up his arm."

Barrett chuckled. "That's sleeve, not arm." Looking back at the screen, they saw that Terd was starting to shake and bounce around the alien's stomach.

"Whoa, that dude's not going to like this!" said Barrett. They saw the creatures stomach walls heaving, and then witnessed Terd's ejection out of the creature's mouth.

"Ooooh!… It's a good thing I didn't eat any breakfast—this is disgusting," said Barrett. Terd fell onto a dry area on the ground again and shook off like a wet dog. They could still see the creature gagging and retreating from the area.

"Terd Reeflaki Tirent Bissca. I ordered Terd to return to the ship. We will need to search for a different Fayron," said Fobo.

Terd was back in the ship and out of danger. He flew over to Fobo and placed his robotic arm into a hole on the cryogenic tube. The stored energy he transferred from the creature to Fobo seemed to be enough to help him regain some needed energy. Fobo began to slowly lift himself out of the glass cryogenic tube he had been in for 102 years. Not completely out, but he now revealed the upper and mid portion of his body. Barrett, not sure exactly what Fobo was doing, asked, "Hey, I thought you had to stay in that thing?"

"My energy increases. Terd has collected enough energy for regeneration," says Fobo. Barrett took a good long look at his new alien friend.

"You know, you're not as creepy-looking as I thought you were, but what's up with beer belly? You look pretty fat for a guy who hasn't eaten in over a hundred years."

"Thanks… I think," said Fobo.

CHAPTER 10

Barrett, Fobo, and Terd were all together inside the ship. Fobo knew that they must find another Fayron as soon as possible. "We will need to return to an altitude of one miset to continue our search."

"One miset it is, Captain," said Barrett, pretending to work the controls. They slowly rose above the jungle canopy, then climbed straight up at an incredible speed. Terd forgot to hang on and fell to the ground, unable to hover due to the "G" forces. Fobo looked at him like he should know better.

They reached an elevation of one miset (two hundred miles) in mere seconds. Terd returned to a hover as Fobo brought up the planet's holographic image. Fobo turned to Barrett. "We will need to find an area with several Fayrons to increase our chances of success," as he pointed to an area on the planet. "This area has three Fayrons within an extremely narrow canyon. Hold on to something, Barrett...you too, Terd."

Barrett and Terd held on tight as the ship proceeded at level flight, then suddenly plunged to the surface. "Geez, Fobo...where did you learn to drive like that... Mars?"

Confused, Fobo reacted. "Barrett, I have never been to Mars—it has no Fayrons."

"It's a joke, Fobo." The ship flew through a deep, narrow canyon, with sharp rock cliffs, strange trees, other plants, and steam that was shooting through fissures in the planet's crust.

"This is awesome! It reminds me of prehistoric drawings I saw in a textbook at school."

Fobo wasn't paying attention and didn't really hear what Barrett was saying. He was worried about something. "I am picking up hostile patterns," he said to Barrett.

"Not one of those creepy lizard creatures again, I hope."

"No, Barrett," Fobo replied. "These patterns are not coming from indigenous life-forms. We need to find somewhere to hide the ship."

Barrett was silent, letting Fobo concentrate on his task. The ship reversed its course and flew through the canyon in the opposite direction of the hostile patterns. Fobo was busy at the controls. He saw a cave near the top of a mile-high cliff face and directed the ship to it. They entered the cave, which was barely big enough to accommodate the ship.

"We will stay here. They will not be able to find us."

"They who?" said Barrett.

"They are known as Trites. The Trites are an evil race, with a voracious taste for Fayrons. They believe that the Fayrons are an aphrodisiac. We have been fighting the Trites for over one thousand of your earth years."

"Wait…a taste for Fayrons!" Barrett exclaimed. "I'm a Fayron! … Does that mean they're going to eat me?"

"Not if I can help it, Barrett," said Fobo. That didn't exactly calm Barrett's nerves.

"I thought you guys couldn't kill anything?" he asked.

"We will do what is necessary to defend ourselves…and to protect the Fayrons."

"So do you have weapons…like ray guns, photon torpedoes, and stuff?" said a hopeful Barrett.

An unemotional, "YES" comes from Fobo.

"Cool, but I guess they do too…right?"

"Yes, Barrett…but we do not have enough energy at this time to defend ourselves adequately. Our best defense is stealth."

Barrett, still uneasy, "Do they have the technology to detect Fayrons…like you do?"

"Unfortunately, yes…but only at very close range."

"How close?" Barrett asked.

"1.3 Fragsets, or about one hundred yards. However, they cannot detect you while you are in this ship."

Barrett looked relieved. "The Trites are very close to the Fayrons. Their patterns are scattering. We will send Terd to investigate."

Barrett was worried and has doubt. "Terd! … but they'll see him, then they'll know we're here?"

"They won't see him, Barrett."

Fobo gave a command to Terd. "Terd...
Fremak Taras Bebaro... Figi-Rim."

Terd made some bleeping noises, then sped
through the ship's hull. Both Fobo and Barrett
watched him on "Terd vision" as he traveled down
the canyon wall, then hovered gracefully above the
surface. He stopped for a moment to get his bearings,
then suddenly sped through the canyon looking for
the Fayrons. Barrett was watching with fascination.
"Go, baby, go!" he said. Terd traveled for about sixty
seconds, then slowed down near a large tree.

Terd was not always controlled by Fobo and
could act autonomously when needed, so he decided
to land near the top of the tree for a better vantage
point. Terd changed his form to resemble the tree
branch he was resting on. Back on the ship, Barrett
and Fobo reacted to what Terd saw. "There it is...is

that the Trite ship? What are all those things running around on the ground…are those the Trites?"

"That is the Trite ship. The small creatures on the ground are called 'Rops,' and unfortunately, they are running for their lives. The Trites have a taste for the Rops as well, but they are looking primarily for a Fayron. At least one of those Rops is a Fayron."

"There are so many of them!" said Barrett.

Terd was staying in place for now as they observe. Fobo focused the range on Terd's camera to get a closer view of what was going on. They saw the Rops scurrying around, jumping into burrows, and hiding behind trees. The Rops were small, almost pancake-shaped, and had short soft hair. They had no offensive capabilities, but this gave them a slight advantage because they could fit into small crevasses. They focused in further and saw the door of the Trite ship open. Three of the Trites exited their triangular-shaped ship with large guns attached to their arms. They literally came out shooting, and were killing many Rops. They were gathering them with what looks like a bayonet at the end of their weapons and placing them in their side bags.

The Trites had some human features. One head, two arms, and two legs, but that was where the comparison stopped. Their skin was reptilian, much like alligator skin. Their mouths were large, with multiple serrated teeth that looked like that of a great white shark. Barrett thought to himself that they looked like a brown version of the Gorn on *Star Trek*.

Barrett was extremely worried about the cute little Rops. "The Rops…they're killing all the Rops!" he said. Fobo was looking down at his control panel.

"We won't be able to save them all, Barrett, but we must at least try to save the Fayron… I have a plan." Fobo gave Terd another order. "TERD... FIGI-RIM ROP."

With that order, Terd flew straight down to the ground and changed his form to look like a Rop. He headed to the burrows that the Rops were jumping into. "That's a great idea, Fobo," Barrett said. Terd wasn't in the hole yet and was dodging laser blasts while probing every Rop that he passed...making them jump up and make noises as if they were Tasered. Terd finally entered the burrow to continue his search.

"This may work...if they haven't killed it yet," said Fobo. They continued to watch Terd in the burrow. Rops were everywhere. Terd kept scanning...so did Fobo.

"We've got one. A Fayron just passed him!" he said with excitement.

Fobo sent an order to Terd again. "TERD. FREMAK ROP!" Terd turned around and chased the fast little Rop through the tunnels in the burrow. He finally cornered the Rop…it was shaking nervously. Barrett was concerned. "The Rop looks scared."

Fobo replied, "Not for long, Barrett." They kept watching as the Rop stopped shaking.

"What did you do?" said Barrett.

"Once it was isolated from the rest of the Rops, I telepathically transferred a message to him.

"Do you mean a suggestion…what was it?" Barrett asked.

"Yes, I suggested that he should come with us to Ramar, where he will be safe from the Trites, and where the female Rops outnumber the males thirty to one."

Barrett smiled. "That's very clever," he said. They continued watching Terd, who was now back to his original form and next to the Rop in the burrow. Terd got closer to the Rop and enveloped it. Now that the Rop was safely inside Terd, he changed back to look like the Rop again.

Fobo ordered him to come back to the ship. "TERD... REEFLAKI TIRENT BISSCA."

Most of the Rops were now hidden safely below ground, while the Trites were on the surface, counting and picking up their bounty. With Terd's order to return to the ship, he left the relative safety of the burrow and scurried across the ground with his precious cargo inside. Unfortunately, one of the Trites saw him escaping. A greedy lone Trite stealthily followed Terd without his or Fobo's knowledge.

Barrett was proud and happy that they were successful in saving the little Rop. "We did it! ...will this little Rop give us the energy that we need to kick some Trite butt?"

"It will surely help our efforts, but we're not out of the forest yet, Barrett," said Fobo.

"That's 'out of the woods,' Fobo."

CHAPTER 11

Terd was in an area that had tall grass, covering him from the Trites' view...he believed. Even with the Rop's energy, he lacked enough power, so to fly, he needed to change back to his original form. The Trite was hiding behind a tree, but clearly witnessed the transformation. Terd became airborne and headed up the cliff face to get back to the ship. The Trite watched him leave and saw him enter a cave near the top of the canyon. He used a neck communicator to alert the other Trites. *"A Ramarian drone is within the canyon,"* he said.

Back at the ship, Barrett was excited to see that Terd was back in one piece. Terd released the Rop and placed it near Barrett. "Good work, Terd! Hey, this Rop is kind of cute," he said cheerfully. Barrett reached over, picked up the Rop, and placed it on his lap. It instantly peed on him.

"Oh crap…this thing just peed on me!"

"That's his way of saying he likes you, Barrett." said Fobo.

Barrett grimaced. "With friends like this, who needs enemies?"

Fobo was still monitoring the Trites. Knowing their tactics well, he was never complacent. The Trites were busy picking up their bags and guns and rapidly running back to their ship. The Trite commander was screaming at his subordinates to hurry. All in, the ship took off. "They are approaching," Fobo said to Barrett.

"Approaching! …you mean they're coming up here?"

"Yes," said Fobo. "If we hadn't brought on this Fayron, we would be sitting geese."

"That's sitting ducks, Fobo...so what do we do?"

"The Trites will not attempt to fight us while we are in this cave. They know we have superior weapons and will likely wait until we leave the cave, then attack us from all sides. They naively think that we don't know they've surrounded us and will exit the cave uncloaked."

"All sides! They only have one ship, don't they?" said Barret.

"I am picking up three ships now." he said nonchalantly.

"You know... Being a Fayron isn't all that it's cracked up to be. Do you have any other enemies that you're not telling me about?" said Barrett with exasperation.

"Isn't one enough? ...the Trites will form a triangular attack configuration. Two below and one above. We must create a diversion before escaping."

"What type of diversion? These guys seem to be pretty smart," he said.

Fobo broke his usually calm demeanor and began to laugh. "Smart!... Trites are known for being one of the dumbest species in the universe. They are primitive beings and have stolen all the technology they possess."

"So what are we going to do?" said Barrett.

"Our ship does not have enough power to completely cloak or change form, but Terd can...here's what we are going to do."

Fobo told Barrett the plan, then called Terd back to him. Fobo transferred Terd back the power that he gave him. Fobo would have less energy, but it was a necessary setback. The Trite ships were coming from several directions, and as expected, formed the attack configuration that Fobo anticipated. Inside the Trite's ship, the commander spoke to the other ships. *"This appears to be a single Ramarian ship. It must be a scout. We will wait until it shows itself."*

Back on Fobo's ship, Barrett appeared worried. "Do you think this will work, Fobo?... I'm kind of counting on it."

"It worked on them before. They are a very curious species and are easily distracted." Fobo continued, "The Trites don't learn from their mistakes."

"Alright...let's do this!" said an excited Barrett.

Fobo ran his hand over the control panel and gave Terd a command. "TERD... REEFLAKI VARIT TRITE KNOKIT." Terd now had enough energy to change and maintain form in flight. He bolted out of the ship, taking on the appearance of an indigenous reptilian winged creature that commonly nested in caves on Tayth. He exited the cave without any resistance. The Trites saw the bat-like animal, but didn't respond. Terd flew past the ships, turned around, and landed on top of the ship that was at the top of the attack configuration. Fobo, watching Terd vision, saw that Terd is in position.

"Terd… Figi," he ordered.

Terd began scratching and knocking at the top of the ship, then flew to the other ships doing the same thing. The Trites were bothered and annoyed by this distraction. All three ships sent scouts out through the hatches to see what was causing the noise. Terd rushed back to the ship and quickly gave Fobo and the ship his stored energy. "He's back!" said Barrett. "It's working…we will try to cloak our ship, but it may not be fully powered to do so…hold on!"

The ship sped out of the cave, only partially cloaked. The Trite commander saw the Ramarian ship leaving the cave and took the first shot. He was unsuccessful. The Trite ships were unable to lock their weapons with the soldiers outside the ship. The Trite commander was furious and screamed for them to get back in the ship, but he didn't wait. He gave the command to intercept the Ramarian ship. All three ships took chase, knocking the Trite soldiers off the ships...falling to their deaths. Fobo's ship had a good lead, but he knew they would follow him. "We're not out of the woods yet, Barrett."

Barrett was shocked that he got that one right. "Hey, you got that one right. Good job, Fobo!"

"The Trite ships are closing in," said Fobo.

"I think it's time to break out the photon torpe-does and ray guns and stuff," said Barrett.

"Our ship is very old, and the weapons have not been tested. We should have enough power soon, but may need to depend on our ability to outthink them."

"Well, if they're as dumb as you say, that shouldn't be too hard...can we make our ship look like one of theirs?" he said hopefully.

"Barrett, you read my mind. We can't cloak, but we should be able to change form," said Fobo.

"As you said, Fobo. Your thoughts have become my thoughts, and my thoughts have become yours... let's kick their alien butts!"

"We will need to do a little fancy flying...hold on, everyone!"

The Trite ships were closing in. Fobo buckled in, and flew directly over the Trite ships. Fobo changed his ship to look like one of theirs. The Trite commander realizes what had happened and could not distinguish his ships from the Ramarian ship.

The commander yelled, *"You are cowards! …show yourselves…show yourselves or die!"*

The Trite commander got no response. All four ships were facing each other in a standoff. *"Then die,"* the commander exclaimed.

Frustrated, the commander ordered his ship to fire on all the ships. *"Kill the cowards…kill them! Destroy all the ships NOW!"* he said.

The second-in-command spoke to his commander. *"Destroy them all?"* He questioned his command. *"I will not, commander—two of them are ours!"* he said in defiance.

Furious, the Commander approached him. *"Then you will die."*

He grabbed him by the head and instantly broke his neck, throwing his body off to the side. He sat in the gunner's chair and prepared for battle. *"Die,"* he said in a sinister whisper, then started randomly shooting at the ships. The first hit was taken by a Trite ship…it was destroyed. The captain of one of the other Trite ships realized that his commander had gone rogue, so he took aim at his ship and fired a shot. The commander fired two shots, but it was too late. Both Trite ships had destroyed each other simultaneously. One shot was also fired at Fobo's ship, but missed. "Yeah…we did it," said Barrett, "they totally fell for it…that's the oldest trick in the book."

"Yes, they fell for it, hook and sinker… I told you they were dumb." Barrett looked at Fobo and decided not to correct him this time. He was happy about the outcome and realized that it could have gone the other way.

"Should we go back to Tayth and get another Fayron?" he asked.

"No, Barrett. Other Trite ships will be arriving soon…and they will be looking for us. We must leave this system immediately."

"Can we go to your planet?" said a hopeful Barrett. "Nothing would please me more, Barrett, but I cannot return to Ramar until my mission has been accomplished."

"Why," said Barrett. "you've got a Fayron… heck, you have two…me!"

"Barrett, a thousand years ago, Ramar was a large, beautiful world, enriched with a thriving Fayron population. Unfortunately, the Trites found ways to infiltrate our planetary defenses, and it took only one hundred years for the Trites to decimate our Fayron population, bringing it to a level where even the smallest planet could not survive. Our ancestors developed more elaborate defensive weapons, and we were able to keep the Trites off Ramar, protecting what was left of the Fayron population. For thousands of years, we held the belief that Fayrons from other planets should not be removed, and should live and die without outside interference, but one hundred and four years ago, in order to keep our planet from dying, the Grand Council allowed for the capture of ten Fayrons. They approved one ship…my ship. It was ordered that if I was unsuccessful, that there would be no second mission. My mission was expected to fail."

"How do you know that they haven't approved another ship? …you have been gone for one hundred and four years!"

Fobo brought up a holographic image of a sun-drenched, dry planet with active sandstorms. "This is Ramar today. If the Grand Council had approved another mission and had it been successful, Ramar would show signs of regeneration."

"I see what you mean…but why don't your people just move to a planet that has a lot of Fayrons?" Barrett asked.

"We do have small bases on other planets, but are unable to populate them with substantial numbers…our ancient Pharah prohibits this."

"What is the ancient Pharah?"

"The Pharah is much like your ten commandments, Barrett. The Pharah laws were written prior to known Ramarian history and are sacred to all Ramarians. Its laws are strictly adhered to," said Fobo.

"You and the Rop must rest now. Sweet dream, Barrett."

Barrett put the Rop in one of the cleaned enclosures, then made himself a place to sleep. Fobo plotted a new course, then entered into inter-dimensional transfer. The ship was again flying through the wormhole.

CHAPTER 12

Back above the planet Tayth, there were twelve Trite ships of different types, flying through the debris from their recently destroyed ships. The Trites' superior commander accompanied and led the squadron. He spoke to the other ships. *"We must find who is responsible for this…these were some of our best ships… FIND THEM!"* he shouted angrily. The Trite ships split up and dispersed in two directions.

Back on Fobo's ship, Barrett and the Rop were sound asleep. Fobo was attempting to get the remainder of his body out of his cryogenic tube. He was weak at first, but gained strength rapidly. Finally, he was out of the tube that had been his home for over one hundred years. He slithered over to a round area which was the secondary pilot's plate. Fobo could run more of the ship's operations from this area.

Barrett was awakened by Fobo's movements. "Where are you going?" he said to Fobo.

"Good morning, Barrett. We must prepare our ship for collection. We have entered a system with many Fayrons."

Barrett got up and looked out the window. He saw several planets surrounding a bright bluish star. "Wow…this is incredible! There are so many planets!"

"This is the Pholop system," said Fobo, "named after its largest planet."

"Which planet are we going to visit?" asked Barrett.

"Many, but the first planet is Pholop." Fobo pointed to a large planet through the window.

"That's humungous!" said Barrett.

"This planet is the largest...even larger than earth and Ramar. Its swamps hold more Fayrons than all the planets in this system combined," he said. Fobo brought up the holographic image of Pholop. The image revealed ninety-eight red dots...ninety-eight Fayrons.

"Ninety-eight Fayrons," he muttered with disappointment. "That is a healthy number, but over one hundred years ago, Pholop had over two hundred Fayrons... The Trites have been very busy in this system since my departure."

"You've been here before?" said Barrett.

"Oh yes...part of my mission was to repair and reestablish a remote Ramarian defensive base that was partially destroyed by a single Trite scout 110 years ago. Fortunately, he was killed in the explosion before he could inform his commander about the location. The unmanned base was very effective at protecting the Fayrons from the Trites, and it was my job to bring it back to its previous glory. I eluded the Trites for over two months while repairing the base and collecting Fayrons. The repairs were almost complete when a Trite ship spotted me outside the safety of the base. Knowing that if the base was found, they would surely destroy it, I led them away from the planet and escaped with four Fayrons."

"Dude… I sure hope they are paying you well," said Barrett, joking. "Do you think they went back and destroyed it?"

"I don't believe so. I repaired and implanted a cloaking device which, if still operational, would make it invisible and undetectable to the Trites." Fobo pointed to the image again. "The base location is here…prepare for landing, Barrett."

The ship went straight down toward the planet. Barrett was holding on with both hands, looking out the window as the ship traveled over the thick canopy of trees. The surface was covered by a bluish fog. "This place is really creepy-looking," said Barrett.

"You haven't seen anything yet...the reptilian creature on Tayth was small compared to some of the life-forms on this planet."

The ship slowed down, then stopped. Barrett was still looking out of the window, in awe of his surroundings. "Why did we stop?" he asked, while turning towards Fobo. Fobo waved his hand over a panel, then turned to the window and pointed his finger.

"Look over there, Barrett." Fobo and Barrett both looked out the window. Out of nowhere appeared the now uncloaked Ramarian base. It looked much like Fobo's ship with convex and concave features, beautiful colors, and clear glass-like domes on the top. Projecting out of the domes were large pointed objects.

"Wow, this thing is huge! …can we go in there?" Barrett asked.

"Yes," Fobo replied.

Fobo paused for a moment. "I am picking up no aggressive patterns in the area." Fobo directed his ship towards one of the round areas at the bottom of the base. A large opening appeared as the ship entered and landed. Once inside, he closed the door behind them. They were now completely invisible from the outside of the base.

"Welcome to my base, Barrett. Make yourself a home."

"Thanks, Fobo…and that's 'make yourself at home,'" said Barrett. The ships door opened. Fobo entered the base with Barrett and Terd following directly behind him. The inside of the base was large, with rounded walls and control panels.

"You Ramarians sure like round things," said Barrett.

"Later in your life, you will see the importance of this," he replied. "But now, we will eat. Barrett, please collect the Rop from the ship… I will prepare food."

CHAPTER 13

Six Trite ships were entering the Pholop system. The Trite superior commander was in the largest ship. He pressed a button on his control panel and spoke to the other ships. "*This is a large system…begin the search. If you find them, kill them!*" he said with an angry, agitated voice. The Trite ships separated in three groups and flew towards three different planets.

Back at the Ramarian base, Fobo was sitting at a round table with Terd above him. Barrett was sitting across from him with the Rop next to him. The table was filled with green, purple, and yellow plants… some are moving. "No way…you don't expect me to eat that stuff…do you?" Barrett said with his tongue outside his mouth.

"Well, the Rop seems to like it," said Fobo, as the Rop engulfed his food. Barrett turned to the Rop and spoke to him.

"Geez, you're grossing me out. Look at you… you're slobbering all over the food!"

"You'd better eat something before the Rop eats it all," said Fobo.

"Yeah…yeah. Alright," he reluctantly conceded. Barrett realized that there are no utensils on the table, so he reached over and grabbed the least offensive food he could find, then took a small bite.

"Hey, this isn't that bad!" he said. Barrett looked over at Fobo, who was also shoveling food in his mouth.

"Boy, all you aliens eat like pigs!" Barrett gave in and attacked his food like the rest of them.

"If you can't eat 'em, join 'em," said Fobo. Barrett just grinned and shook his head.

CHAPTER 14

One of the Trite ships was flying over the planet "Tara," shooting their lasers at anything that moved. A herd of two-headed "Lakmas" were running away from the laser blasts. Inside the Trite ship, the Trite captain was laughing and having a great time killing the creatures exclusively for sport. The superior commander's ship came out of the haze and over the captain's ship…seeing and hearing him. He spoke to the other ship in a sarcastic tone. "*Captain…with all this laughter, you must be celebrating?*"

"*Um… No, Commander!*" said the captain. "*We just thought th—*"

The commander interrupted him. "*Don't think, Captain…find the Ramarian ship that destroyed our ships or die!*"

Dutiful, the captain agreed. "*Yes, Commander,*" he replied.

Barrett and the gang had finished their meal. Fobo raised his head and spoke to Barrett. "We must repair more enclosures in the ship to prepare for our new Fayron guests." Fobo and Barrett got up and walked back to the ship. Fobo began calibrating the ship functions as Barrett headed over to the largest enclosure. He opened it and started removing some of the bones from the enclosure's floor. He reached deeper inside a dark area and grabbed something. He pulled it out and realized that it looks like a human skull. "Fobo, is this a human skull?"

"A humanoid, Barrett," he replied. Barrett instantly dropped the skull on the floor, breaking it in pieces.

"You are troubled, Barrett?" he asked in a conciliatory manner. Barrett clearly had a worried look on his face.

"Am I going to die too?" he asked breathlessly.

"Barrett…are you afraid of dying?" Fobo said in a calm voice.

"Of course, aren't you?" said Barrett.

"Dying is a regeneration of life and should not be feared."

"I guess it's the fear of the unknown," Barrett said.

"Facing the unknown will make you stronger, Barrett."

Barrett replied, "Yeah, I guess so," as Fobo left the ship.

"Where are you going?" he said. Fobo turned back and faced Barrett. "To get a few Fayrons…are you coming, or are you afraid?"

Barrett's fear turned to excitement. "Yeah, I'm coming…count me in!" Fobo and Barrett walked to another room toward the rear of the base. They entered the room and saw two round disks on the floor.

"What are these?" asked Barrett.

"These are our transportation disks…unless you would rather walk?" said Fobo. Barrett looked outside through a window and saw the slimy swamp water. He turned to Fobo.

"Disks…disks are good," he said. Fobo stepped onto a disk as Barrett followed his lead.

"I have a skateboard, so this shouldn't be that hard," said Barrett. On the disks, they began to raise off the floor.

"Follow me, Barrett."

"Wait, how does this thing work?" asked Barrett.

"Just think about where you want to go. The disk will read your thoughts."

"You guys are really into reading minds," he replied. Fobo opened the door and drove his disk out of the base. Barrett followed closely behind, still a little unsteady. Terd followed.

They were moving rapidly just above the swamp surface with Terd following directly behind. "This beats skateboarding, hands down!" Barrett was clearly enjoying himself.

"I've always enjoyed flying these things. Stay close. A Fayron should be near."

They traveled several miles away from the base when Fobo's sensors started lighting up. Fobo came to an abrupt stop, as does Barrett and Terd.

"The Fayron is below us," he said to Barrett.

"Where…in the water?"

"Yes. I will send Terd down there. Stay very still." Fobo sent a message, and Terd splashed down into the water. For a moment, it was quiet, then Terd popped up out of the water right next to Barrett, startling him.

"Whoa… Terd, you scared me!"

"It is moving. We will follow." The creature was moving, disturbing the water on the surface in front of them. They slowly followed it through the swamp, when Barrett saw something break the surface of the water.

"Hey, Fobo, did you see that? it's over there!" he said, pointing to the left of Fobo. Fobo sent Terd in the water again, then brought up Terd vision which could be seen at eye level on each disk. "Alright! … underwater Terd vision!" says Barrett. They could see Terd traveling through the water. Many strange fish and amphibian type creatures were all around. Suddenly, they saw what looked like a big tail that was flapping back and forth. "There is our Fayron, Barrett. He is too large for Terd to collect. We will continue to follow it."

"This thing looks like a snake," said Barrett.

"Looks can be deceiving...this is a Hissoru. It is not indigenous to this planet and is an intelligent plant and insect-eating creature." Terd popped out of the water, as the snake-like Hissoru slithered up a tree in front of them. The Hissoru wrapped itself around the tree while moving its head from side to side in a defensive posture. Its eyes were locked on Fobo as it started hissing. From the neck down, the creature looked much like a snake, but had four hand-like fins on either side of its body. Its head had a small mouth and eyes that looked much like Fobo's.

Fobo whispered to Barrett. "Be silent… I am communicating." The Hissoru stopped hissing and appeared to be silently communicating with Fobo, when suddenly, it dropped back into the water.

"Where did it go?" Barrett asked. Fobo put his finger to his mouth as if to tell Barrett to be quiet. Almost a minute passed when the Hissoru jumped out of the water, directly in front of Barrett. Barrett screamed and fell backwards into the water. "Aaaahhhh! Get me outta here!"

Fobo was laughing as he stuck his tail in the water to help Barrett. "Let me help you up, Barrett." Barrett pulled himself up with the assistance of Fobo's tail. He managed to get back on the disk, but had swamp slime all over him.

"Oh, man… I hope you have a shower back at the base."

Fobo, still laughing, "I think you scared the Hissoru."

"I scared him? …what about me?" said Barrett. The Hissoru was back in the water, with just his eyes cautiously peeking up through the water as it moved closer to Fobo.

Fobo introduced Barrett to the Hissoru. "Hissoru, Barrett. Barrett, Hissoru." Barrett looked at the creature while brushing the slime off himself.

"Hello…it's a pleasure to make your acquaintance, Mr. Hissoru," he said.

"We will go back to the base…the Hissoru will follow."

The Trite superior commander had left the planet Tara and was flying towards Pholop. Two other ships had joined him.

CHAPTER 15

Fobo, Barrett, Terd, and the Hissoru entered the Ramarian base. "Barrett, stay here… I will return in a moment."

"Wait, are we going to get more Fayrons today?" he said with Fobo's back to him. Fobo turned.

"Yes, but first I would like to show you something." Fobo took the Hissoru into the base and showed him around, then returned to Barrett. "Follow me, Barrett." As before, they both got on their transportation disks with Terd following close behind.

"Where are we going, Fobo?" said Barrett.

"One day, when I was searching for Fayrons, I found something. Something amazing. Now I will share it with you." They continued the trip through the swamp, when Fobo started to slow down.

"Are we here?" Barrett asked.

"No, Barrett, I am picking up hostile patterns… we must hurry!"

They started moving again. Unfortunately, as fast as they were going, the hostile entity seemed to be making headway and was approaching rapidly. "It is getting closer," said Fobo.

"What's getting closer?" he said. Just as he asked, a massive creature the size of a four-story house came out from behind a huge rock. It looked like an upside down octopus with eyes and horns at the end of each extremity. Its legs were submerged under water, but it could move rapidly.

"Oh my gosh…what the heck is that?"

"Don't move, Barrett. This is an Octhorn. Octhorns are known for their aggression and angry disposition, but lucky for us, they have very poor eyesight."

"Bad eyesight! ...but he's got eight of them!" said Barrett.

"That's why they are so angry. As long as we are motionless, it should not be able to detect us."

The Trite ships had arrived on Pholop. One ship was just above the canopy scanning for Fayrons very close to Fobo's location. Fobo and Barrett were hiding and doing their best not to make any noise. The Octhorn was knocking down trees in its search of Barrett and Fobo.

"Oh no!" said Fobo quietly.

"What now, Fobo?" Barrett and Fobo heard a humming sound, then saw the Trite ship above the trees.

"Barrett. Stay behind this tree. The disks do not have a cloaking device." Barrett squeezed in next to Fobo, as close as he could to get cover by the large tree.

Inside the Trite ship, it was the same Captain that was reprimanded by his commander for shooting creatures on planet Tara. He saw the Octhorn and couldn't resist the temptation to kill it. *"Look…an Octhorn! …the Superior Commander will not deprive me of this kill."* The other Trites on his ship were all smiles and just as excited as he was. They began firing on the Octhorn. Fobo and Barrett were watching the battle.

"Oh my gosh, I almost want the Octhorn to win," said Barrett.

"We must use this opportunity to escape," said Fobo.

"Are we going back to the ship?" Barrett asked.

"We cannot risk leading them to our base…follow me." Barrett, Fobo, and Terd quickly retreated away from the Trite ship and the Octhorn.

The battle between the Trite ship and the Octhorn continued. The ship was just out of reach of the Octhorn's hard poisonous horns on its long tentacles. It was less of a battle and more like a massacre. They shot several shots directly in the center of the Octhorn, killing it almost instantly. They were celebrating their kill, when one of the Trites saw the disks fleeing. *"Captain…look! A Ramarian disk!"*

The captain was smiling. *"This is a good day… kill them!"* said the captain. The Trite ships began firing at Barrett and Fobo. The chase was on.

"Use full power, Barrett, and follow me," he insisted.

The Trite blasts were getting close to them, but the Trite ship was too large and needed to stay above the tree canopy, giving Fobo and Barrett a slight advantage. Fobo began flying in an S-shaped pattern, making it more difficult for the Trites to hit them… Barrett did the same as Terd followed.

"Where are we going?" said Barrett.

"You will see," he said. Ahead, Fobo spotted a familiar area with large old hollowed out broken trees, which were remnants of an ancient forest that had been taken over by the swamp. Fobo, Barrett, and Terd were dodging laser blasts as they headed for the old trees. The Trite captain was having a hard time keeping his eye on them due to the dense foliage.

Fobo tried his best to speak to Barrett. "Do you see the large broken tree next to the large rock?" He pointed his finger ahead of them.

Barrett shook his head in the affirmative and said, "Yeah."

"The tree is hollow. When I say 'now,' fly the disk into the top of the tree… I will follow."

"You're the boss, Fobo," said Barrett.

"Remember, not until I say 'now!'" They were travelling very fast. Fobo gave Terd an order.

"TERD… REEFLAKI TACHI BAKLA TRITE." Terd flew back into the water and picked up some swamp slime. He cloaked, then flew straight up, behind, and then over the Trite ship. Terd was now above the ship's command bridge window. Fobo saw that Terd was ready and in position. He waited for just the right moment, then gave the order to both Barrett and Terd.

"FIGI… NOW!"

Inside the Trite ship, the window was suddenly drenched with swamp slime. The Trite captain couldn't see anything and was having a hard time controlling the ship. He was hitting tree after tree.

Barrett didn't see what happened and was just concentrating on getting to the top of the hollowed out tree. He reached the top and dove directly inside the tree, but Fobo didn't follow and appeared to have driven right past the entrance to the tree. Barrett yelled, "Fobo…come back…come back!"

Barrett paused and now understood what Fobo had done. Reluctantly, he lowered himself down inside the dark hollow tree. Fobo was still flying and found a clearing, waiting for the Trite captain to see him. The slime was off the Trite ship's window, and he could now see clearly. The captain looked out the window and saw Fobo. *"Well, there's one of them. Attack!"*

They began chasing Fobo again. He was moving fast and was leading the Trite ship as far away from Barrett and the base as he could. He was still flying back and forth in an S-pattern, waiting until he could find just the right moment when the Trite ship couldn't see him. Fobo directed his disk into an area with heavy cover from the thick canopy. With the Trite ship momentarily out of view, he quickly jumped into the swamp, sacrificing his disk as it exploded after hitting a large boulder. The Trite captain saw the explosion. *"One down…we will find the other…these Ramarians are known for being stupid."*

Barrett was still inside the tree. He didn't hear the hum of the Trite ship and believed it was safe, so he slowly raised his head out of the top of the tree and saw that there was no one around. "Fobo… Terd!" he yelled, without thinking of the consequences. Barrett ducked back inside the tree, realizing that yelling was probably not the best thing to do.

Terd was cloaked and was flying low through the swamp, then splashed down into the water to look for Fobo. After a few moments, they both popped up out of the water together. Terd was extremely happy to see Fobo and couldn't control his emotions. "Bleep…bleep…whistle," he said to Fobo.

"I'm fine, Terd. Go to Barrett. REEFLAK TANI BARRETT." Terd flew off as Fobo swam rapidly through the water. He came up to a huge fallen hollow tree and entered the opening.

Barrett was sitting quietly on his disk just below the inside top of the tree when he heard a noise. Worried that the Trite ship was coming back, he cautiously peeked over the top of the tree to take a look. As he did, Terd popped up at the same time and scared Barrett. "AAHH! Geez, Terd. You love scaring me…what happened to Fobo?"

"Bleep…ping…ting," said Terd.

A sarcastic Barrett replied, "You don't say… you've got to learn English, dude." Terd went down into the tree, passing Barrett.

"Terd…where are you going?" Terd faded into the darkness of the hollow tree. Barrett decided to follow him down the tree, tearing his shirt sleeve on a splinter of wood as he did. They were in almost complete darkness, except for Terd's blinking light and the disk's dull glow.

"Terd, don't go down there. There might be a monster or something." Terd came back to Barrett and touched a button on the disk. A small headlamp popped out and illuminated the inside of the tree. At the same time, a light came out from the top of Terd as well. Barrett was amazed at what he saw. The inside of the tree was massive, with statues of humanoid type aliens everywhere.

"Wow, this is so cool, Terd! Does someone live here?" he asked, knowing he wouldn't get an answer. Terd made a few noises, then headed down a hollow root tunnel. Barrett reluctantly followed.

"I hope you know where you're going, Terd." They continued down the root tunnel when Barrett heard something.

"Terd, stop," he orders. Terd stopped and Barrett passed him to investigate. Not knowing what to expect, he proceeded with caution. His light was illuminating the walls of the tree when he heard a voice. "Hello, Barrett!"

Barrett screamed again while moving his light to see. "Awe... Jesus H Christ, Fobo... I think you guys get some kind of perverse thrill out of scaring me to death."

Chuckling, Fobo reacted. "Sorry, Barrett." It was obvious that they did enjoy scaring him.

"How did you get in here... I saw you fly past the entrance?" said Barrett.

"Most of these ancient trees are interconnected. After losing the Trite ship, I entered a fallen tree and followed a root tunnel to get here. This is what I wanted to show you."

"What is this place?" asked Barrett. "Does someone live here?"

"This is what's left of an ancient alien civilization. We know very little about them, except that most of their lives were spent within these hollowed out trees."

"This place is incredible!" He changed the subject. "Hey…where's your disk?" he asked.

"It was destroyed," said Fobo.

"Are you okay?"

"I am fine, Barrett, but we must get back to the base, collect the Fayrons, and leave the planet. They know our approximate location. We can't risk them finding the base."

Fobo and Barrett got on the remaining disk and headed back to the base with Terd following close behind. Just as they left, several dozen of the "extinct" humanoid-like aliens popped their heads out of from several hollowed out stumps to watch them depart.

CHAPTER 16

Just above the cloud cover, the Trite captain was joined by the Trite superior commander's ship. They were communicating on screen. *"So, you said that you killed one Ramarian…where is the body?"* said the superior commander.

"Commander…we saw the disk blow up, so we assum—"

The superior commander interrupted. *"Never assume, Captain. No body, no kill…take me there,"* he said incredulously. The captain followed his orders and led him to the crash site.

Barrett and Fobo were still racing towards the base. "Barrett...they are coming back. Take an eye out for the Trite ship," said Fobo.

"Fobo...that's 'keep an eye out.'" The Trite ship was high above the canopy, but passed Fobo and Barrett without detection.

"It appears that the danger has passed...for now," said Fobo. "but we must hurry."

The two Trite ships were hovering over the area where the Trite captain saw Fobo's disk blow up. The superior commander ordered the captain of the other ship to investigate. "*Go down there, Captain...find your kill,*" he ordered. The Trite Captain entered the ships docking area and found a Ramarian disk that was stolen from a former battle with the Ramarians. He opened the door and exited the ship on the disk. Hovering over the crash site, he saw what remains of the disk, but saw no evidence of the dead Ramarian. He searched the area around the site, but again found nothing. Touching a button on his neck communication device, he nervously spoke to his superior commander.

"Superior Commander... I do not see the body."

Hearing this, the superior commander opened communications to include the other ship while turning the captain's communicator off. *"Leave him to rot in the swamp scum,"* he said defiantly. Both ships departed, leaving the Trite captain behind.

The captain on the surface raised his arms and yelled, *"I will show you... I will redeem myself!"*

Fobo, Barrett, and Terd approached the base and enter. Fobo stepped off the disk and turned to Barrett. "Barrett. Dock your disk and bring the Rop to the ship. I will get the Hissoru and meet you there." Rushing, Barrett docked the disk, but failed to securely lock it on the docking pad, leaving a portion of the disk sticking outside the base. Barrett touched a button on the wall next to the door to close it and walked away, not knowing that the disk was partially visible from the outside.

The Trite captain had not given up and continued to look for clues to find out what happened to the Ramarians that were flying the disks. He began by looking for any spot where they could be hiding...behind large rocks and trees, searching several areas around the crash site. After searching for over thirty minutes, he saw the large hollowed out tree and decided to investigate. Looking for an opening, he flew to the top of the tree and looked in. He saw nothing at first, then something caught his eye. He reached down and picked up a small piece of fabric... the torn piece of Barrett's shirt. After searching deeper inside the tree, he found no more clues or signs of life. Although he was reluctant to leave without finding any bodies, he decided to fly the Ramarian disk in the direction of his departed comrades.

Barrett was back in the ship holding the Rop as Fobo and the Hissoru slithered through the door. Fobo, again, looked worried. "The Trite ship is approaching…we can't leave until they are out of this sector," he said.

Barrett responded. "We're safe in here, right?"

"As long as the Fayrons stay in this ship, they cannot detect us."

"Cool," said Barrett. Fobo ordered Terd to cloak and to go outside to give them a view of the Trite ships. Fobo and Barrett were both watching Terd vision and saw two Trite ships directly over the base as another one joined them.

"There they are, Fobo!" as the color was drained from Barrett's face. "They know we have Fayrons… they will try scanning for them." They continued to watch. Barrett looked worried.

"If they find us, we can defend ourselves, right?" he asked of Fobo.

"The cloaking device also serves as a protective barrier or shield against the Trite's weapons…it can withstand a significant amount of direct fire. The base also has a very powerful weapon system. When activated, it can autonomously fight off dozens of ships, even when there's no one in the base."

"Dude, then activate the friggin' thing…we'll kick their butts!" said Barrett with a hopeful tone.

"I had hoped to have enough time on the planet to re-activate the automatic defense system, but it doesn't look like that will be possible."

Discouraged, Barrett replied. "Great! …we're sitting ducks."

"Well, not completely, Barrett. The base weapons can be operated manually…and our ships weapons should now be functional as well. We will use these only as a last resort."

"Come on Fobo," Barrett replied, "I have a BB gun at home, and I'm a great shot! I say we bury the sum-bitches!"

The Trite ships were still over the base, but started leaving one by one. "It looks like they're leaving," said Barrett.

"It appears that way, but we will wait until the coast is cleared."

"That's 'coast is clear,' Fobo."

They stayed in the ship for several more minutes, until they were confident that the Trites have left the area. Fobo sent Terd above the trees to investigate. They looked in all directions on Terd vision and saw nothing. Confident, Fobo ordered Terd back into the base.

CHAPTER 17

The Trite captain was on the disk, flying approximately two feet above the swamp surface. He was furiously looking for either the Ramarian or his Trite counterparts. His search was thorough and lengthy, and he was determined to not leave any stone unturned. The sun was starting to fade as he saw something glowing about fifty yards away. He cautiously flew close to the glowing object and saw that it was a section of a Ramarian disk. Confused, he slowly flew around it to look at the other side, but bumped into the invisible base wall. Talking to himself, *"I have found it! I have found the Ramarian base!"*

Proud of his find, he tried to contact his superior commander. *"Superior Commander... I have found the Ramarian base and weapon!"* He got no response and realized that they have likely turned his device off. *"Damn... I will do this myself,"* he whispered. He reached down to check his belt. It was loaded with weapons. He pushed a button on one of the objects on his belt.

Fobo was concentrating on the control panel and noticed something a little off. Confused, he spoke to Barrett. "I am picking up strange patterns."

"Great...what is it this time?" asked Barrett. Fobo didn't answer as he was busy working.

The Trite captain stepped off his disk and walked over to the still glowing partial disk. He touched the disk and moved his hand around the edges. As he did, his hand went through and became invisible. He pulled his hand out and again tried to reach his commander. *"Superior Commander... I have infiltrated the Ramarian base...do you hear me?"* Again, he got no response. Knowing that if he alone could seize or destroy the base and its defensive weapon, he would be considered a hero and would be honored, gain rank, and adorned with medals and great wealth. He again put his hand inside, followed by his head. Looking in, he saw the large room. It was difficult, but he managed to squeeze his body through the small opening.

Fobo was still inside the ship, while Barrett, knowing that the enemy was gone, was just outside the ship looking in at Fobo. Fobo suddenly yelled out, "Barrett, we are not alone... GET BACK IN THE SHIP!"

Unfortunately, it was too late. The Trite captain grabbed Barrett and held a sharp round object to his neck. Barrett was caught off guard and screamed.

Fobo looked at the Trite and warns him. "Do not hurt him, Trite!" he said in the Trite's language. The Trite spoke, but Barrett did not understand his language.

"Ah…a human…and a Fayron as well. He will be very tasty. Thank you, Ramarian."

"What's he saying, Fobo?" Barrett asked.

"Do not worry, Barrett," he said, trying to calm him down.

"Take me to the weapon," the Trite insisted.

"Release the human first, Trite," said Fobo.

"I will not…show me the weapon or I will kill him!"

Fobo paused and thought about his options, then called Terd. "TERD… REEFLAKI TACHI BAK TRITE." Terd responded immediately. He came from the back of the base at full speed, slamming into the Trite's head, knocking him unconscious onto the ground. Barrett was unharmed.

"Yay, Terd…you got him!" said Barrett.

"He must be a Trite spy," said Fobo.

"Do you think he told the other Trites about the base?"

"Yes…the object on his neck is his basch, a communication device. I will turn it off…we must leave as soon as possible."

The three Trite ships were flying in formation. Inside the ship, the communications officer was talking to the superior commander. *"Sir, I intercepted this transmission from Captain Zeel."*

"Read it to me," said the commander.

"Superior Commander… I have found the Ramarian base and weapon," said the officer.

"Did you try contacting him?" asked the superior commander.

"His Basch is turned off."

"Do you have the location?" he asked.

"Not yet sir, but we should have it in short order," The communication officer said with his head bowed down towards the floor.

"You better," insisted the superior commander.

Back at the Ramarian base, the Trite was tied up on the floor, and all his devices and weapons had been taken from him and laid out on the floor. Barrett put the Trite's communication device around his neck and grabbed his weapon belt…about to put it on. "Hey, Fobo, how does this look…pretty cool, huh?" he said.

"That must not be tampered with, Barrett. It is very dangerous." Fobo slid over to Barrett to look at the belt.

"Look, it's got all these blinking lights and stuff," said Barrett.

"Blinking lights!" said Fobo, concerned.

"It may be an explosive device." Fobo reached over and took the belt away from Barrett. "As I thought. It is set to explode in forty-two seconds."

Barrett was still shaken. "Can you disarm it?" he asked.

"No time…we must get rid of this now!"

Fobo called Terd again. "TERD REEFLAKI TERSWA BAKHIM RAPPI." Terd flew over to Fobo. Fobo put the belt around Terd with only twenty seconds left. He flew through the base wall and was travelling over the swamp as fast as he was capable of doing. He was about five hundred yards away with just four seconds to go when he dropped it in the water. He quickly reversed his direction and started his way back to the base when it exploded, throwing him against a tree and dropping him in the water.

At the base, they felt the concussion of the blast which awakened the Trite captain. Fobo and Barrett were looking for Terd through the window. "Where's Terd," said Barrett, concerned. "He should have been back by now."

"I am getting no readings from him," said Fobo.

"Let's go find him," said Barrett.

"We cannot. The Trite ships are near."

"We can't leave Terd out there, Fobo!"

"It is not my wish to leave Terd, but I must protect the Fayrons… I have no choice."

"But I do," said Barrett under his breath.

"Barrett. You have forgotten that your thoughts are my thoughts. You must not go out there." Barrett reluctantly agreed, but Fobo looked at him with doubt.

"We are out of time, but before we leave, we need to secure the base and find out how the Trite entered."

Fobo approached the Trite captain. "Trite…tell me how you breached the base walls?" he said to the defiant captain.

"*Never! You Ramarian fitch!*" he replied.

Fobo turned to Barrett. "Barrett…you must look for the breach. I will attend to the Trite."

Barrett said "Okay," then proceeded to search the base. The superior commander was waiting to hear from his communication officer when he saw smoke from the explosion miles in the distance. "*I believe we may have found our forgotten captain,*" he proclaimed to his crew.

Barrett was looking all over the base for some kind of breach, but hadn't found anything. He headed to the transportation deck and saw the problem. He shuddered to think that this whole incident and losing Terd was all his fault, so he quickly opened the door to secure the disk that was clearly sticking out of the base. He was just about to close the door when he saw the Trite's disk outside. He ventured outside to bring it in, when his guilt seemed to get the better of him. Barrett approached the disk and for a moment, contemplated on what to do next. "I'm sorry Fobo... but I've got to go look for Terd. He is gone because of me," he whispered under his breath. Barrett jumped on the Ramarian disk and took off in search of Terd.

Fobo was pulling the Trite captain into the ship when he stopped suddenly and looked up. "No, Barrett...no!" he said loudly. He felt Barrett's guilt, but didn't think he would leave the safety of the base to go look for Terd.

Barrett saw the smoke and headed for it, hoping to find a functioning Terd. He arrived at site and immediately started probing the shallow water with his hands. He saw something shiny next to a tree.

"Found you!" Barrett reached out and grabbed Terd's broken arm.

"Terd, can you hear me?" he said. He got no response, so he picked him up and placed him on the disk. Barrett secured him between his legs and raced back to the base. Just as he was leaving, the Trite ships arrived.

A Trite helmsman saw the disk. *"Commander! There's the Captain!"* he said mistakenly.

"That's not the Captain, you idiot!" said the superior commander.

"Should we kill him?" said the helmsman. The superior commander contemplated his next move as his second-in-command entered the bridge.

"No... I don't think he's seen us. Take one of the disks and follow him. Don't let him see you." he said to his second-in-command.

"Yes, Commander," he replied. The Trite officer exited the ship on a disk and stealthily followed Barrett. Barrett arrived back at the base with Terd. He entered the door and parked his disk.

Unfortunately, the Trite soldier saw everything and quickly reported back to his commander. *"Commander... I have found the cloaked Ramarian weapon station. A human Fayron is inside and he is wearing the Captain's Basch around his neck."*

Fobo entered the transportation area and spoke to Barrett. "Barrett...hurry! Close the door!" he said with urgency. Barrett reached over and pushed the button. The door closed.

"I'm sorry, Fobo... I just couldn't leave Terd behind," he said.

"A Trite followed you to the base, Barrett. I must show you how to fire our weapons."

The Trite second-in-command returned to his ship and entered the bridge. The superior commander spoke to his crew. *"Trites…prepare for battle!"*

CHAPTER 18

Both Barrett and Fobo were now in the bubble dome weapon station at the top of the base. Barrett was sitting at the base of the weapon in a chair that was clearly designed for Ramarians, not humans. Barrett turned to Fobo, saddened by what he had done. "I'm sorry, Fobo," he said. "it's my fault that they found the base.

"I am not angry, Barrett," he replied. Fobo leaned closer to Barrett to give him instructions on how to aim the weapon. "Do you want to learn how to use this?" he said.

"Okay, Fobo, I'm ready. Show me how to do this."

"It's very easy," said Fobo, "This is your sight, and the firing mechanism is here," pointing to something that looks like a joystick. "All you need to do is turn your head in the direction of the target and fire. The dome interacts with you and automatically turns in the direction that you look."

"This is the coolest thing ever!" said Barrett.

Suddenly, the base was rocked by a Trite laser blast, followed by another. "Oh my God!" said Barrett.

Fobo put his hand on Barrett's shoulder. "Don't worry, this base can withstand many direct hits. Take aim and fire, Barrett. I will do the same from the other dome." Fobo left Barrett's side and slithered to the connecting Weapon Dome, still close enough to watch and talk to Barrett.

The Trites were now firing from all directions. Barrett saw the ship and began firing. He was spinning around, but missing every shot. "Fobo, I can't hit them!" cried Barrett.

"Close one eye," yelled Fobo. Barrett closed one eye and fired, hitting one of the ships. He aimed again, but the ship exploded before he got another shot out.

"Yeah! Woooo. I got one!" Fobo sat but did not fire. He was watching Barrett with a smile on his face. He thought to himself, *Barrett's got this*, so he got up off his chair and returned back to the ship.

The Trite ships were shooting while moving in circles, making Barrett dizzy, but he kept firing. "I got another one!" he said. There was only one ship left: the much larger superior commander's ship.

"I am not beaten that easily... I will get my revenge," said the superior commander. He was clearly angry and not used to defeat, but knew that he was

now alone and no match for the Ramarian defensive weapons. He reluctantly ordered the withdrawal.

Barrett saw that the larger ship was leaving, so he took aim and fired. The shot missed the ship as it disappeared in the clouds. "Damn, I missed him," he yelled to Fobo.

"The big ship is gone." Barrett looked at the other dome, but Fobo was gone. Barrett got out of his chair and left the dome to go find Fobo.

Fobo was back in his ship, making some adjustments. The Trite captain was on the floor with his back against the wall. Barrett saw the Trite as he entered and ran over to him. "Hey, you lizard head Trite trailer trash! Your buddies are all gone, and I kicked their stinking butts off this planet," he said proudly. The Trite just sat there, not knowing what Barrett has said. Barrett lifted his basch communicator from his neck to his mouth.

"Run away, buttheads," he said into the turned off basch. Fobo turned to look at Barrett.

"You are quite the shot, Barrett," he said with pride.

"How come you didn't shoot 'em too?" said Barret to Fobo.

"It wasn't necessary…you were doing fine on your own."

"Yeah, I was, huh?" he said, smiling.

"So what do we do now?"

"We must leave. Many more ships will come."

"But if we stay here, we can fix the base… I can fight off those stupid Trites."

"This weapon cannot get into the Trite's hands," said Fobo. "I have already started a self-destruct sequence that will destroy the entire base. We can rebuild another base at another time. We must focus on collecting more Fayrons and returning to Ramar."

Both Fobo and Barrett prepared for takeoff. All the Fayrons and Terd were back on the ship, as well as the Trite captain. They did a final inspection and took off. Barrett stood looking out of the window as they entered space. "I'll never get sick of this. I always wanted to be an astronaut, Fobo."

"I know, Barrett," said Fobo with a smile on his face. They both were looking out the window when the base exploded with what looked like a small atomic blast. There was nothing left.

CHAPTER 19

The superior commander's ship was alone in space, over a hundred miles above planet Pholop. He watched Fobo's ship leave the planet and witnessed the explosion of the Ramarian base. He kept his distance but followed the Ramarian ship. *"The base is destroyed. Keep a safe distance…we do not want the Ramarian to know we're following him. We will wait until just the right moment, then attack. Remember, a dead Fayron tastes just as good as a live one,"* he said to his crew.

Meanwhile, Barrett was sitting on the floor with Terd on his lap. He was trying to fix him under

Fobo's guidance. "You must put the red wire into the blue slot."

"That just seems wrong, but okay....now what?" asked Barrett.

"Now, pick up the square ribna and place it into the round fahr," instructed Fobo.

"The square what...into the round what?" He figured it out and realized that Fobo was now sending him instructions telepathically.

"Oh, this?" he said.

"Yes," said Fobo. Barrett placed it in and Terd came to life. Barrett was elated and felt like Doctor Frankenstein. "It's alive!... It's alive!" he said.

Off to the side of the ship, the Hissoru was sniffing the Trite and hissing loudly. The Trite captain was still tied up and was helpless against the Hissoru. *"Get this thing away from me!"* screamed the Trite captain.

"What did the Trite say?" asked Barrett.

"Oh, nothing important," he shrugged.

"Let's just say that the Trites and the Hissorus have a long tumultuous history."

"Oh, come on…tell me," he said.

"Trites have always disliked the Hissorus because of a certain body function that they possess."

"What!" said Barrett.

"Hissorus like to spit on Trites…and only on Trites. It is very irritating to their skin."

Barrett found this amusing. "Really! No way… why?" he asked.

"Many years ago, the Trites attempted to hunt the Hissorus for sport on their home planet of Perth. The Hissorus only defense was their skin-irritating saliva. They could spit this out from quite a distance, much like the spitting cobra on Earth. This proved to be very successful against the Trites, and they quickly retreated. The Hissorus never forgot the siege."

"No way…you're making this up," said Barrett. The Hissoru began to wiggle and squirm, raising his head up like a snake about to bite his prey.

"Look at the Hissoru, Barrett."

The Trite captain knew what was about to happen and yelled, *"Get away from me!"*

The Hissoru was bobbing his head from side to side, then spat. The Trite was suddenly covered with a green foamy slime. *"Ah! Get this stuff off me!"* he screamed.

"Oh my gosh…that is totally sick," Barrett said while laughing. Fobo was laughing as well.

"I have actually never seen this before. It is quite rewarding." They enjoyed watching the Trite squirm as the Hissoru seemed to be gearing up for another round.

"Barrett, you'd better put the Hissoru back in the holding area before he does it again," said Fobo.

"What are we going to do with the Trite, Fobo?" asked Barrett.

"I know of a very special place where we will release him." Barrett assisted the Hissoru into his quarters, then returned to the bridge. Fobo was looking at a holographic image when Barrett walked in.

"Barrett, this is the planet, Tara. Over three quarters of this planet is covered by water. The rest is ice, sand, and rock."

"Does it have a lot of Fayrons?" asked Barrett.

"Yes," Fobo replied. "Most of its Fayron populations are in its thriving oceans, but we are looking for a being found in the ice cap, near the planets northern pole. She is over three hundred years old."

"You know who the Fayron is?" questioned Barrett.

"Yes…she is a 'Shimmering.' Her energy is equal to that of one hundred Fayrons. She is a rare hermaphrodite being that has the ability to give birth to multiple Fayrons without losing her energy…but she has not done so for almost one hundred years. She should be entering another bacul phase soon. If she chooses to come with us, we will need no more Faylons."

"Why do you call her 'She' if she's a hermaphrodite?"

"This is a distinction of her choosing. I respect her wishes."

Fobo ran his hand over the controls and thirty-nine red dots appear on the planet. Five Fayrons were seen on dry land, thirty-three were in the oceans, and only one at the northern polar cap. Barrett pointed to it. "Is that the Shimmering?"

"That is my hope, Barrett. Prepare for entry," said Fobo.

Fobo flew the ship down to Tara's ice cap. It was a treacherous landscape, with jagged ice mountains and unstable moving ice sheets. "How could anything live out there?" asked Barrett.

"Life can exist in much harsher environments than this. Many creatures live on and within these icy mountains and caves. It is a very healthy planet."

"Inside?" questioned Barrett.

"The Shimmering must be nuts to live here."

"Nuts!" Fobo said, aghast.

"The Shimmering is a fantastic being with the wisdom of time. She has lived on many worlds in her three hundred plus years, but has chosen Tara as her home. I came to her over one hundred and two years ago to ask her for her help, but she could not leave Tara."

"Can't you telepathically suggest that she come with us?"

"I cannot," said Fobo. "If she comes with us, it must be her idea."

The superior commander's ship was over planet Tara as nine other ships joined him. He sat in his command chair and spoke to the other ships. *"Trites…the Ramarian ship has entered the northern ice caps of Tara. This Ramarian ship is responsible for the destruction of five of our ships. We will send in only one scout ship… mine. I will signal all our ships when we are ready to take our revenge."*

Fobo took manual control of his ship and was flying directly toward a large pointed ice mountain. "I hope you know there's a giant mountain right in front of us," said Barrett.

"This is the Shimmering's home," he said.

"Oh great…it looks really cold, and I left my jacket back on earth!"

"You will not need your jacket, Barrett."

Fobo's ship entered through a large crevasse within the ice mountain. The superior commander witnessed the entry through a long-distance viewer. The Trite ship was still far enough away so the Ramarian ship could not detect him.

Fobo's ship was traveling through the ice crevasse, and Barrett was standing close to the window with his mouth wide open, in awe of what he saw. The ice was reflecting a rainbow of translucent colors in every direction. "This is the most beautiful thing I think I've ever seen," said Barrett.

"I guess she's not as nuts as you thought," said Fobo.

"Yeah, I can see why she doesn't want to leave."

"Yes...it makes my job much more difficult," said Fobo.

Ahead in the distance, Barrett saw a bright light. "What is that, Fobo?"

"That is her...the Shimmering."

The ship approached the bright light and landed on a flat ice shelf directly in front of it. "We will go now."

"We?... I'm going out there?"

"Of course. I need you to be there. Come with me," said Fobo. Fobo and Barrett walked out of the ship, leaving Terd, the other Fayrons, and the Trite behind. Fobo walked ahead of Barrett. Barrett's eyes had adjusted, and he began to see the Shimmering's shape. She was still brightly glowing, but he could see that she was round and undulating, with her skin reflecting what was around her...including himself and Fobo. They were slowly getting closer.

"Hey, she kind of looks like the Blob...have you seen that movie?"

"She is much more beautiful, Barrett," said Fobo.

"Oh, it sounds like someone's got a crush on the Shimmering," Barrett said with a little chuckle. Fobo did not respond. They were now only feet from her when she spoke.

"Fobo, It's been a long time," she said.

"Hey, she spoke English!" said Barrett.

"It is good to see you again," said Fobo.

"You brought a human Fayron…he is beautiful." She paused…"Your planet is well now?" she asked.

"I am afraid not," said Fobo. "I was unsuccessful in my mission."

"You are here for help, Fobo?" she asked.

"I am…my planet's survival depends on my mission. I have lost valuable time," he told her.

"Fobo…you are a beautiful race and my regrets have been many, but I have chosen this planet for my final years."

"If that is your decision, I will respect it. It is known that you are entering into Bacul soon and will birth several offspring. Our people would embrace, love, and protect you and your young should you decide to change your mind."

CHAPTER 20

The Trite superior commander had separated from the other ships, but gave them an order. *"Captains. The Ramarian ship has entered a cave. I will fly in alone, luring them toward the exit…they will be close behind. When you see me exit, fire all your weapons at the ice around the exit. We will crush them and bury them alive!"*

His second-in-command responded. *"This seems very risky, Superior Commander. Why don't we just fire on the mountain now and trap them inside?"* he suggested.

"We cannot take the risk. There may be other exits. This is the only way assure victory," said the superior

commander. The commander readied his crew and began his decent into the ice crevasse.

Fobo tried his best to convince the Shimmering, but she had made her decision. Fobo was clearly sad-dened by the Shimmering's choice to stay on planet Tara, but knew he could not do anything about it. He had tried this before…unsuccessfully. He told her that he understood, and they said their goodbyes.

Suddenly, Fobo realized that they were not alone. The Shimmering sensed that there was some-thing wrong. "You look worried, Fobo," she said.

"We may be in dan—"

Before he finished, a shot was fired from the Trite ship, hitting the ice above the Shimmering. The Trite ship did not get any closer and did not fire again. The superior commander knew he didn't have the firepower to go against the Ramarian ship alone and wanted Fobo to follow him out to where he was most vulnerable. Fobo turned toward Barrett. "To the ship…get back in the ship," he said with authority. Barrett ran towards the ship, but the Shimmering did not move.

Fobo spoke to her. "You must get in the ship… they will destroy you," he begged.

The Trite commander took one more shot…he was impatient. Barrett looked out the door and saw that Fobo was still talking to the Shimmering, so he ran back to them. He got behind the Shimmering and tried to push her. "I won't let them kill you!" he shouted. Under the circumstances, the Shimmering was very calm.

"I will go…thank you, human," she said to Barrett. The Shimmering rose and seemed to defy gravity as she moved to the ship. Barrett was right behind her and was fascinated by her ability.

"Wow, you aliens never cease to amaze me," he said.

They all entered the ship and the door closed behind them. Fobo turned the ship around and fired one shot at the superior commander's ship... it missed. The commander quickly retreated as Fobo followed him. "Get him, Fobo! Kick his butt!" said Barrett.

"This is unusual behavior for a Trite. He is planning an ambush."

The Trite commander was dodging fire, but trying to keep Fobo's ship as close as possible. He spoke to the other ships. *"The Ramarian ship is following me...prepare to fire!"* he commanded.

Barrett turned to Fobo. "What do we do now?" he said. Fobo was getting telepathic messages from the Shimmering...he looked at her and smiled. Fobo could see the light coming from the exit to the ice cave with the Trite ship in front of him. With seconds to go, Fobo turned his ship through another crevice.

"Hold on, everyone," he said. He picked up speed while looking for an opening.

"There it is," he muttered to himself. He made a quick left turn and found himself back in the original crevice, but now he was in front of the Trite ship, with the exit right in front of him.

With the Shimmering inside, Fobo's ship was functioning at full capacity, so he cloaked the ship immediately. The Trite superior commander did not see him and still believed the Ramarian ship was behind him.

Fobo was just about to exit the cave, then changed his ship to look like the superior commander's ship.

The Trite ships above saw the superior commander's ship exit and begin firing at the ice mountain with everything they had. The mountain collapsed into a giant pile of broken ice. The Trite ships had unknowingly buried their commander's ship as Fobo flew right past them. Once behind the Trite ships, Fobo cloaked his ship again and sped away from the planet.

Inside the ice mountain, the superior commander's ship was crushed by large ice boulders. The defeated superior commander was barely alive, but had just enough life in him to speak a few words. "*You were a worthy opponent,*" he said…then died.

The spirits were high in Fobo's ship. "I told you they were stupid, Barrett," he said.

"These are your enemies, Fobo?" asked the Shimmering.

"The Trites are the enemy of all living crea-tures," he told the Shimmering.

"You and the human have risked your lives to protect me and have shown tremendous bravery, courage and kindness… I would consider it an honor to bear my young on Ramar," she said to them. She was a wise being and knew that Fobo didn't realize he was being followed by the Trites. He would have never exposed her whereabouts if he knew.

"You are indeed a wonderful being…thank you, Shimmering," he said with a bow.

"And thank you for showing me the way to get in front of the Trite ship. It is you that saved our lives, Shimmering."

Fobo turned to Barrett. "Buckle up…we have one more stop before we reach Ramar."

Fobo brought up a holographic image of the sur-rounding planets and aimed his ship at a small planet within the same system. They quickly approached it. Barrett was looking out the window. "What are we going to do here… I thought you had enough Fayrons?" he said to Fobo.

"This is the planet, Perth," he said.

"Wait, isn't that the Hissoru's home planet?" said Barrett.

Fobo smiled. "You are a very good student, Barrett." The ship entered the atmosphere and landed on a small island.

"This looks like a good place for the Trite," said Fobo.

"Yeah, it's pretty…almost too good for the Trite," he said. The door opened, and both Fobo and Barrett escorted the Trite to the beach and placed him near a tree. They untied his legs, leaving his arms bound together. Barrett looked up in a tree and saw a Hissoru.

"I see what you are doing, Fobo…you're brilliant and maybe a little evil!" Fobo did not say a word, but turned his head to Barrett, smiled, and winked his eye. Without another word, they got back in the ship and flew away.

The Trite kicked off a branch to use as a sharp object to cut the rope from his arms when he heard something. He looked at the tree behind him and saw the Hissoru, then noticed about a dozen of them coming out of the ocean, slithering towards him.

CHAPTER 21

Fobo's ship was coming out of the wormhole. Everyone was looking out of the window…even Terd, when they entered the Ramarian system and saw the planet Ramar, distinguished by its two unique purple moons. Barrett looked over at Fobo who had a tear rolling down his face. "Is this Ramar?" asked Barrett.

"Yes… I thought I would never see it again."

"It is still a beautiful planet, Fobo," he said. "Thanks to all of you, it will be again."

They watched in silence as the ship passed through the clouds and dust. Below, they saw thousands of round buildings which Barrett thought looked like Bubble Wrap. There was a large round building in the center of the city. Fobo steered the ship towards it. As they got close, a round door on the building began to open. Fobo's ship entered to thousands of Ramarians making a grunting noise in appreciation of his safe return.

"Fobo, it looks like they knew you were coming," said Barrett.

Fobo just said, "Yes."

The ship landed and Fobo, Barrett, Terd, the Fayrons, and the Shimmering all exited the ship. They were met by the Grand Ramarian, who was holding the "Pharah" tablet. Fobo approached him and bowed down to him. "It is I that should be bowing to you, Fobo," said the Grand Ramarian. Fobo raised his head and stood upright. The Grand Ramarian held out the Tablet and Fobo placed his hands on it. As he did, it began to glow. The crowd erupted with more grunts while slapping their tails

on the ground. Barrett was clapping and grunting along with them. The Grand Ramarian handed off the Pharah and picked up a small silver box. He reached in and pulled out a golden ball, then spoke to Fobo.

"Fobo… Ramar owes you a debt of gratitude. The Grand Council and the beings of Ramar are proud to honor you with the Award of Pharah. With your acceptance, a seat on the Grand Council is yours." He handed Fobo the golden ball.

"I accept the award, and the position of council," he said. The crowd again went crazy.

Fobo looked over at Barrett and reached out his hand. Barrett walked over to Fobo and grabbed his hand. Fobo turned to the Grand Ramarian. "Grand Ramarian. It is my wish to escort the human back to his home planet of Earth. If it were not for him, we would not be here today," he asked.

"Granted," said the Grand Ramarian.

"But, Fobo," said Barrett, "you'll need me to stay here... I'm a Fayron. You can use my energy to help your planet."

"I appreciate that, Barrett," said Fobo, "The Shimmering shall provide us with all the Fayron energy we will need to restore our planet. I made a promise to you that I cannot break."

Disappointed, Barrett replied, "Fobo...it's okay. I want to stay."

"We may meet again someday, but your mother and Kimmie need you more than I."

Later that day, Barrett and Fobo were in an airfield, being escorted to a new ship by two Ramarian diplomats. The field was filled with onlookers, the Shimmering, and the Grand Council. They entered the ship, but not before turning around and waving to the crowd. Fobo got in his seat—something he didn't have in his ship—and prepared the ship for takeoff. It was quite different than his ship, but he figured it out. The large dome door started to open.

"Would you like to drive, Barrett?" he said.

"You bet!" said Barrett, "how?"

Fobo exited the chair and pointed to it. Barrett wasted no time getting in. "Just look to the stars and wish it. Giv'em what you got, laddie," he said in a terrible Scottish accent. Barrett looked at Fobo and corrected him for possibly the last time.

"That's giv'er all you've got, Fobo."

"Yeah, that's what I said," said Fobo. Barrett smiled.

"Wait, where's Terd?" he said.

"Oh, I almost forgot. Go ahead, call for him, Barrett." said Fobo.

Barrett felt like he knew enough of Fobo's language to give the order. "Terd Reeflaki," said Barrett.

Terd came directly through the hull of the ship and landed in Barrett's lap. "Nice to have you back, Terd." Barrett smiled and looked up at the stars.

"Let's go home."

CHAPTER 22

Barrett was in the cave back on earth and was sleeping next to the sewer pipe. He was awakened by John and Ladd shining a flashlight on him. "Dude, what are you doing down here? We've been looking all over the place for you!" said Ladd.

"Wow…what time is it? I can't believe I fell asleep," said Barrett.

John, looking upset, said, "It's late man…you were supposed to sleep at Ladd's house tonight… what were you thinking?"

"Ah…leave him alone. He probably just wanted to talk to the sewer pipe again," said Ladd.

"Let's go," said John.

The two boys turned back and crawled out of the cave. "I'm right behind you," said Barrett. Barrett picked up his flashlight and pointed it at the sewer pipe.

"This couldn't have been a dream," he whispered. He got up to get out of the cave when he felt something on his neck. He grabbed it and looked down.

"It's the basch communicator… I knew I wasn't dreaming." He hid the basch and exited the cave where John and Ladd were waiting. He decided to never tell anyone about this, as he knew they would think he was crazy.

Barrett hasn't seen Ladd or John for over ten years. Ladd ended up as a computer science teacher, and John joined the army and is a sergeant with a large family. The date with Kimmie went really well. They stayed together through college and finally got married. Barrett's studies led him to NASA, where he worked as a flight control specialist, but then ventured off for a higher position.

We again see forty-year-old Barrett sitting on his porch. It is still dark outside. His wife, Kimmie, joins him and sits down. They sit quietly, looking up to the stars and the two purple moons of Ramar.

The End.

About
the Author

Chris Doohan is the son of the late James Doohan, who portrayed Montgomery "Scotty" Scott on the original *Star Trek*. Chris himself appeared as an extra in *Star Trek: The Motion Picture* in 1979 and later had roles in J.J. Abrams' *Star Trek* and *Star Trek: Into Darkness* as a transporter room officer. Chris also portrayed Scotty in the award-winning web-based fan production *Star Trek Continue*s, voiced Scotty for *Star Trek Online*, and has performed on several audio books. He grew up in Van Nuys, California, is married, and has two grown daughters. In his professional life, Chris spent over thirty-five years working as a registered vascular technologist. Chris currently resides in Thousand Oaks, California.

CPSIA information can be obtained
at www.ICGtesting.com
Printed in the USA
JSHW060001130523
41616JS00002B/12